Personal as Puck

Lowball Bay Sea Dragons
Book 2

Freya M. Love

I want to thank all the women who came before me for their generosity, and all of those who come after me for their energy. And Heather Hilenbrand who changed my fucking life.
And last but not least, Olivia, for being the best damn friend a bitch could have.

Note from the author

To my beautiful sisters who have struggled with fertility issues, I want to give you the warmest and most gentle of hugs, and a warning that this book contains mentions of infertility. Please look after yourself and your mental health, and know you're amazing and I see you!

With love, Freya.

Introduction

He's five years younger than me, and he's determined to get under my skin. And my lycra.

Nate Southwell and I have nothing in common, except a love for hockey and getting sweaty. Me, in the gym, as a personal trainer. Him with every puck bunny he can get his hands on.

What could the defenseman for the Lowball Bay Sea Dragons possibly want with me? Does he want to add me to his list of conquests?

That must be it. I have a better chance of being run over by a peddle-powered car driven by pink monkeys than have this be real love.

Right?

To add to the mess that is my life, a blast from the past has shown up to turn everything on its head. Don't even get me started on my eccentric grandmother.

I might lose my pucking mind, or I might end up falling head over heels, in spite of myself.

Tropes: Reverse age gap, fake relationship, one bed, playboy, opposites attract, workplace

Chapter One

Oaklyn

A SHIRTLESS DEFENSEMAN, GLISTENING WITH sweat, was the first thing I saw when I walked into work on Monday morning.

"Nate Southwell, you're in my gym again." I unlocked my locker and tossed my bag and keys inside. I closed the door and turned around to lean against the cool metal. A stark contrast to the heated look he was giving me.

"Hey." He grabbed the towel that was hanging over the handlebar of the stationary bike and wiped sweat off his forehead and handsome face. "I like it better in here."

"What's wrong with the players' gym?" I asked.

This one was intended for use by staff who

wanted to exercise before or after work, or while on lunch break. It was smaller and basic compared to the Sea Dragons players' gym. Of course, for Lowball Bay's professional ice hockey team, nothing but the best would do.

Nate grinned. "It's full of players."

I raised my eyebrows at him.

Rumor had it, that description fit him perfectly. Player on and off the ice. Exactly the kind of guy who had a woman like me running for cover. Not to mention the fact he was a good five years younger than I was.

He threw the towel over his shoulder like it was a leather jacket and he was a movie star instead of a professional athlete. I tried to ignore what it did to my lady parts.

"I know what you're thinking," he predicted.

"What's that?" I immediately stopped thinking about how it would feel to have him undress me slowly, and thought about something unpredictable instead. Why was toothpaste mint flavored? Wouldn't it be more fun if it was chocolate flavored? Although, chocolate-fresh breath might not be as nice. Maybe something else, like lemon.

"You're wishing I'd ask you out," he said.

I pushed myself off the locker and walked over to

straighten the weight stand. "If we placed a bet on you knowing what was going on in my head, you would have just lost."

"What would we have offered as a wager?" He stepped away from the stationary bike and over to one of the treadmills.

He was only a couple of feet closer, but he might as well have been standing right beside me. His presence in the space almost knocked the air out of my body. A fact he was no doubt aware of. Men like him knew how they affected women. He knew all the right moves to get what he wanted.

Unfortunately for him, I had no intention of becoming one of his conquests. No matter how much my pulse ratcheted up around him. In a week or two, someone else would catch his eye and he'd be off again.

"What makes you think I'd wager anything?" I asked, trying to act disinterested.

He cocked his head. "Are you trying to tell me you don't have a competitive streak like me? Because I know you do. I can tell."

I nodded my satisfaction at the perfect alignment of the weights, and stepped away, putting more distance between me and him.

"Maybe I do. What would you have bet, Mr.

Defenseman? Let me guess, the loser has to clean the roller coaster at Lowball Bay pier with a toothbrush."

Nate laughed. "No, but I'll keep that in mind next time I make a bet with one of the guys. It'd be funny as hell to see Cam North scrubbing the whole ride, inch by inch." He mimed meticulously cleaning the air right in front of his eyes.

"I'm sure Andi would love that," I said sarcastically. Andi Welling owned the team, and was dating the winger.

"Andi would laugh her ass off," Nate said. "Then she'd probably help him."

"That sounds about right," I agreed. "She wouldn't want him to suffer alone." The pair were head over heels for each other. They were sweet to watch, although they might give me cavities if I was around them too often.

"For the record, I'd bet a date with you." He stepped onto the belt of the treadmill and pressed on the display to get it started. "Your turn, what would you have wanted if you won?"

I ignored the question. "Why would you want to go out with me? There's thousands of single women in Lowball Bay closer to your age. Maybe even some you haven't gone out with yet." By 'going out with,' I meant 'slept with.'

What he did in his spare time, with his body, was his business. I wasn't going to make it mine. Guys, especially ones like him, didn't stick around, not for women like me. No, it was better if I didn't go there to start with.

He stopped and stared at me, apparently forgetting he was on the machine.

"I— Shit!" The treadmill slid him backward and threw him off the end. He staggered and windmilled his arms to keep from falling on his ass.

"Why wouldn't I want to go out with you?" Nate asked as though he hadn't almost crash landed on the hard floor. "You're beautiful. And smart and sexy. You deserve to be taken out and spoiled rotten."

I gave him a look to remind him to be more careful on the exercise equipment. "You hardly know me." If he did, he'd be the one running for the hills.

"I'm a good judge of character," he declared. He all but vaulted back onto the treadmill and resumed jogging without missing a beat.

"Me too," I told him pointedly.

"Ouch." He winced. "If you really are, then you'd know I'm a good guy. Ask anyone. Except Zack Reed, but he hates everyone. No one's gonna accuse him of being a good judge of character."

As far as I could tell, Zack hated himself more than he hated everyone else, but that wasn't a conversation I was going to have with Nate.

"Being a good guy doesn't immediately qualify you as boyfriend material." I watched his expression carefully.

I doubted he was after a relationship that lasted longer than a few hours, much less long enough to be considered a boyfriend. Throwing around words like that might have the desired result. He'd move on and stop pretending he was using the staff gym to get away from the rest of the team. He was here for one reason and one reason only. To get into my pants.

He was out of luck. There wasn't room in my lycra for the two of us.

He didn't flinch. "Of course it doesn't. A position like that requires a lot of work, not just being nice." His deliberate choice of words wasn't lost on me.

I ignored the way my clit suggested I move over closer and maybe lick the sweat from his bare torso. That was not going to happen.

She sulked in response.

"You have experience in that department?" I asked.

"Let's just say I've been practicing," he hedged.

"But a guy can't practice forever. Sooner or later, he's going to need some ice time."

I tucked some stray hair behind my ear and moved over to straighten the yoga mats.

Three days a week, I held yoga classes during lunch break. I'd miss them when this job ended. Working in Sea Dragons Arena was amazing, but I was only here for six months. Just until Lacey was back from having her baby. After that, I'd have to figure out where I was going next.

"You get lots of ice time," I told him. "Hitting that ole biscuit into the basket on the regular." Never the same basket twice.

"I might spend more time working on my stick skills than you think," he suggested. "Since I met you, I've let my puck skills get a little rusty."

"I'd be very concerned if they get rusty after only two weeks," I said dryly.

Don't think about his cock, I told myself. *Lemon toothpaste. Lemon toothpaste. Lemon toothpaste.*

He chuckled. "Me too. Which brings me back to our date."

"We don't have a date," I said. "Except an expiry date, which I think has already passed."

"I like living on the edge," he said. "Besides,

everyone knows expiry dates are just a guide. Eating something after that date is totally fine. Delicious." His gaze dropped to the apex of my thighs. "And if it kills me, I'll die happy."

"If you want to drink spoiled milk and make yourself sick, that's up to you," I said, pretending to misunderstand. "I know when it's best not to step over a line."

Even nudging it with my toe never went well in the past. Those days, it was easier to stay far away from it. On the sidelines, where I belonged. In the back of the stands with a big tub of popcorn.

Also, I wasn't thinking about him licking my pussy now. Not at all. Except maybe a brief thought. Very brief. Super brief. Barely a blink.

Should I give in, sleep with him and let him move on? No doubt I'd enjoy myself. Would he though? Maybe I'd disappoint him. Then I'd have to endure his sympathetic glances every time I saw him. Or look for another job sooner.

No, I definitely shouldn't go there. He'd move on soon enough, and so would I.

"Did you just call yourself spoiled milk?" he asked, looking offended on my behalf. "If that's how you see yourself, then you really need someone to take you out and show you a good time. You're better than that. How long has it been since someone got you flowers?"

My whole body stiffened. Bad memories threatened to flood my mind. Memories I tried so hard to put behind me.

My voice tighter than I intended, I said, "I can buy my own flowers if I want flowers. I don't need flowers."

He must have caught the expression on my face, because he slowed the treadmill and stepped off carefully. He approached me with just as much care in his steps. "Of course you can. I just meant—"

"I knew what you meant," I said.

I started to apologize, but stopped. If this was what it took to put him off, let him think I was a grumpy bitch. It might be what he needed to walk away and not look back. "You and I, we're not going to happen. I mean it, Mr. Defenseman. We won't. We can't. End of story. Full-time."

"I always thrived in overtime," he said softly. From the set of his stubbled jaw, he wasn't going to back down or give up. Not without trying for more shots at goal. What would it take for him to grab his things and walk out my door?

I could tell him to fuck off, but that wouldn't be a good look for an arena employee. Speaking like that to one of the players could get me fired, especially if he gave the arena management an ultimatum. If they had to choose between him and me, he'd win every time. He must have known that.

"I think you're in the wrong position," I said. "You should play offence instead of defence."

"You should have been a goalie. Nothing gets past you." He grabbed his towel again and wiped his face. I tried to ignore the way the sweat trickled down his lean, toned body.

"Sometimes it does," I said. "We can't save every shot."

"There's a saying that you miss every shot you don't take," he said slowly.

"If I thought you wanted more than just to get into my basket—" I started.

The glass doors leading out of the gym were pushed open, cutting me off mid-sentence.

A security guard stepped through, a girl of about sixteen years old behind her.

"Oaklyn Walsh? This girl says she's with you." The guard jerked her head towards the girl, who pushed her backpack up her shoulder and lifted her chin.

"I *am* with her," she stated.

I looked at her sideways. I couldn't remember

having ever seen her before, but there was something familiar about her. Something I couldn't put my finger on.

"I'm sorry, I—"

"I'm Cadence Walsh," she declared. "I'm your sister."

Chapter Two

Nate

The resemblance between them was obvious, now I looked more closely. Oaklyn and Cadence had the same golden blonde hair, although Cadence wore hers shorter. Both had the same blue-green eyes. Both wore the same puzzled expression that contrasted with their flared nostrils. They seemed to be sizing each other up.

"Well, this is...nice," I said to break the silence. "I'm Nate Southwell." I offered my hand to Cadence.

She glanced at me with all the disinterest of a sixteen-year-old. "Hey." She turned back to Oaklyn.

I lowered my hand. Not everyone was a fan, I guessed. "So, what brings you to the arena?"

Oaklyn hadn't said a word, she was still staring at

her sister, her face pale, tinged with an interesting shade of green. Should I get her a pail, or push her in the direction of the restroom? She looked like she might lose her last meal.

I have to admit, even now, like this, she was absolutely gorgeous.

"I came to find my sister," Cadence said. She seemed to have a lot more to say than that, but didn't elaborate.

Oaklyn shook her head. Her full lips moved. For a moment I thought she was going to say she didn't have a sister. Her posture suggested denial, with a hint of fight or flight reflex, edging towards flight.

"Maybe we should all sit down?" I suggested. "It seems like you two have things to say to each other."

They both contradicted me by saying nothing.

Okay, if they needed a mediator, I was down for that. Anything to stay in Oaklyn's company a few minutes longer.

Working out in the staff gym so I could see her a couple of times a week wasn't enough. Convincing her I wasn't just trying to get her into bed had proven difficult so far. More than difficult, if I was honest, but I wasn't going to stop trying, not yet. No one ever said I was a quitter.

"I'm guessing it's been a while since you've seen each other," I started. "Am I right?"

I looked from one sister to the other. Hoping one of them would kick start the conversation between them. I was used to dealing with stubborn people, but usually they were my teammates. How difficult could this be though? A beautiful woman who was apparently immune to my charms, and a teenager.

I had this.

"We've never met," Cadence said. "I'm not sure she even knew I existed. If she did, she never made an effort to get to know me." Her delicately pointed chin was raised higher now, anger flashing in her eyes.

"I knew you existed," Oaklyn said softly.

Cadence's hands fisted at her hips. "Then why didn't you try—"

"Do you have any idea how difficult everything was?" Oaklyn's hands were also in fists.

"Of course I do, but you could have tried." Cadence's face turned pink now.

"You obviously have no idea..." Oaklyn shook her head, making her ponytail swish back and forth.

"You two look so alike." I grinned.

They both turned to glare at me. Okay, maybe I

didn't have this. At least they were united in their irritation at me. That was some kind of a win, right?

I raised my hands to either side of my face, in surrender. "Sorry, but it's true. You're obviously related."

And right now, the way Oaklyn was looking at me was hot as hell. Her eyes flashed and the color was back in her face. This was the most emotion I'd seen from her since I first laid eyes on her here in the staff gym.

The second I met her, I was one hundred percent gone. Every other woman on the face of the planet ceased to exist. The more she tried to keep me at arm's length, the more intrigued I was. One way or another, I'd get through to her. To make her see the real me, not just my reputation. Okay, my *past*, but it was just that, in the past. I was different now, because of her.

"Why don't we all take a step back and breathe for a moment?" I suggested.

I wasn't wrong about them having a lot to say to each other, I was certain of that. The question was, could they clear the air without feeling like they were sticking fingers into what were obviously open wounds? Maybe more than a finger; a thumb, then twisting it around all the way.

I needed to proceed with caution.

Oaklyn took a literal step back and shook out her hands to release the tension. "It's complicated."

"It's not that complicated," Cadence said. "Let me make it easier for you. Mom and Dad are both dead. Car crash." She let out a sigh through her nose and swallowed down a knot of emotion. Her eyes glazed, but she blinked hard a couple of times before the tears could slide down her cheeks.

Oaklyn's face snapped back toward her sister as though she'd been sucker punched.

"Dad is dead?" Her voice wavered. A whole bunch of emotions flickered over her face. Denial. Surprise. Hurt. Even a hint of relief in there somewhere.

Yeah, it was definitely complicated.

Cadence shrugged. "I thought you would have known. Do you even care?"

"I haven't spoken to him in years," Oaklyn said. "If my mom knew, she didn't tell me."

"If your..." I trailed off and flicked a finger back and forth between them. "You don't have the same mother?"

Cadence rolled her eyes at me. "Give the guy a gold star," she said sarcastically.

"I'll take a gold star," I said with a smile.

Everyone had their price, and apparently that was mine. I also enjoyed cake.

She muttered something that sounded like, "Why am I not surprised?" under her breath.

"No, we don't have the same mother." Oaklyn's tone was tighter than the laces on my ice skates. "Our father left my mother for hers."

This was clearly an old pain she'd clung to for quite a while. One that was raw and bitter. I wanted to pull her into my arms and hold her, her face pressed to my chest just over my heart. If I did, chances were I might not let her go again.

Personally, I was okay with that, but I had a feeling she wouldn't be. Not yet. Not until she was ready.

"He shouldn't have bothered," Cadence said. Apparently bitterness didn't fall far from the tree.

"Let me get my shirt and we can go to the café," I said.

The coffee they served here at the arena was almost drinkable. Even if it wasn't, they needed to sit down and have this out.

"You should go to morning skate," Oaklyn told me absently.

I didn't get the impression she wanted me to go

away. She seemed concerned about me getting into trouble with Coach.

"I have time," I said without glancing at my watch.

I was invested in this situation now. There was no way I was going to walk away and let them deal with it alone. Not with Oaklyn hurting as badly as she clearly was. And the kid? I kinda liked her. She had sass. If Coach didn't like it, I'd handle him too.

Call it a family emergency if you wanted to. They were family and one day Oaklyn would be mine, making Cadence my sister-in-law, more or less.

See, definitely a family emergency. Coach would understand.

Without giving them a chance to argue, I trotted over to snatch up my T-shirt from where it hung over a weight bench and pulled it over my head. Before I could yank it all the way down, I caught a hint of regret in Oaklyn's eyes, her gaze lingering on my abs.

Yes! I was finally getting to her the way she got to me. My heart did a little happy dance, and my balls and dick weren't far behind.

I reminded them we were in the presence of a sixteen-year-old, and they managed to contain themselves. For now, because being around Oaklyn made it difficult. Just looking at her made me diamond hard. How could I not be? The woman was a goddess. Some day, I'd make her see that.

I straightened the hem and offered both of them an arm each, elbows bent.

As I expected, neither of them hooked their arms through mine and walked beside me. Instead, Oaklyn gave me a look and headed out the door, leaving me to follow, with Cadence on my heels.

Okay, I would have liked to touch Oaklyn, but this way I got to admire the curve of her ass in her lycra instead. I wanted to cup her cheeks with my hands and give them a squeeze.

I was tempted to slap her ass and make her skin pink, but I suspected she might slap me back, and not the cheek on my ass either.

No, I'd wait until she was ready, and she would be. However long it took, I'd wait. Oaklyn Walsh was mine, whether she realized it yet or not.

Also, you know, not in front of a kid. Even I knew that.

"Are you going out with my sister?" Cadence asked, falling in beside me.

"No, he is not," Oaklyn said over her shoulder.

"Not yet," I said. "I'm still working on her. Your sister is as stubborn as she is beautiful."

"She's smart," Cadence said dryly. "Everyone knows men are trouble."

"Ouch," I said, pretending to be offended. These sisters aimed right for the heart. "Okay, I admit, some of us are trouble."

She lowered her face and looked at me from between her eyebrows. "I wasn't born yesterday."

I couldn't help grinning. She was blunt. I liked that in a person. I never had to worry where I stood with someone like her. If I did something to piss her off, she'd come right out and say so.

"Okay, maybe more than some of us are trouble, but some of us are worth it." I'd make Oaklyn see that, no matter what it took. She'd be worth every minute of the wait, and then some. Even if that wait was so long my balls turned blue and left my body out of sheer frustration. They never had to be patient before, but for her they would be. It wasn't like they had a choice, being attached to me and all.

We followed Oaklyn into the café and sat down at a table near the window. On this side of the stadium, we only had a view of the street, but my eyes were on the woman who sat across from me.

Cadence slipped into the seat between us and leaned back, arms crossed over her chest. All pure attitude.

"So you two are half-sisters," I said, trying to break the ice and get the conversation moving.

"Another gold star," Cadence said. "I'm impressed."

She was clearly not impressed.

"Cut him some slack," Oaklyn said. "He's only trying to help." She didn't look all that impressed either, but I didn't think it was aimed at me. Rather, at the situation she found herself in. What started off as a regular workday had quickly gone sideways.

On the other hand, now she was sticking up for me? This day was looking up for one of us. That 'one of us' being me, in case you didn't realize. Although, she was one step closer to coming around to my way of thinking, so maybe she was winning as well.

"Yes, we're half-sisters," Oaklyn said on a long breath.

"Your parents broke up, then your father got together with Cadence's mother?" That happened often enough, but I got the impression he'd walked out on his daughter as well as his partner.

Or was there more to the situation that I was understanding?

"No," Oaklyn said softly. She stopped while the server came over to take our orders. Ignored me when I said I'd pay, and paid for her and Cadence's glasses of juice.

When the server left, she said, "My father got together with Cadence's mother before my parents broke up."

Chapter Three

Oaklyn

16 YEARS EARLIER

Why does being a woman have to be so painful?

My lower lip firmly jammed between my teeth, I swung my bag over my shoulder and walked out of the school gates. My bag smacked into my back a couple of times before I slipped my arm through the other strap.

I straightened up and winced. All I wanted to do right now was curl around my stomach and try not to die.

Okay, that was melodramatic, but my period hurt.

Ever since the first one, I swear it was getting

worse. Every month, the pain became more intense. Or maybe I was just over it, and my tolerance was lower..

I pressed a hand to my forehead over my eyes to protect them from the midday glare. I had a hat, but I hated wearing it. I was fifteen, I had a hairdo to protect. So my hat stayed in the bottom of my bag, the tag still attached.

A small part of me wished I had a bike so I could get home sooner. On the other hand, the very idea of riding with intense pain trying to rip my stomach apart made it hurt even worse.

Luckily, home was only a couple of blocks away, through the suburbs of Seattle. Suburbs that were quickly getting colder as winter approached. Good, I loved the cold. I liked nothing more than to curl up under a blanket and watch a movie. Or read a good book. Preferably a romance.

Let my mother roll her eyes; I ate them up. I was a sucker for a happily ever after. Some day, when boys were less icky, I might have one myself. My perfect man was tall, dark, handsome and romantic. He'd bring me flowers like my father did for my mother. Every single Friday after work, he brought home a bouquet.

Okay, most Fridays. A couple of times recently,

he forgot, but he seemed to have a lot on his mind. He'd always tell me not to worry about it, that it was grown-up stuff.

I stopped at the first set of traffic lights to wait for it to change. Like always, when I wanted to get home in a hurry, it took its sweet time. So long I was tapping my foot on the pavement when it finally did change.

I shuffled across the road, half curled in over myself. Silently, I reminded myself to put some painkillers in my school bag for next time. I'd had a packet, but I finished the last of the pills last month.

I stepped onto the opposite footpath just as the traffic started moving again. The thrum of the cars at my back, I headed down the block.

A white SUV pulled up in front of a house, maybe a hundred feet ahead. The doors opened and people started to climb out.

A man took a stroller out of the back of the car, while a woman opened the door and pulled out a small bundle. In her arms, she cradled a tiny baby, swaddled in a pale pink blanket.

I was only half paying attention until I was a few feet away.

I stopped dead.

Stared.

Blinked a couple of times to make sure I wasn't seeing things or losing my mind.

The woman placed the baby into the stroller and smiled down at her fondly before kissing the man on the mouth. "I'm glad you were able to be with us today, to bring her home. You're always so busy, I thought maybe..."

"I know," he said with a sigh. "Soon, I'll have more time to be here with you and our daughter. I need to—"

"Dad?" The word slipped out of my mouth.

He looked over at me, startled. The only way I can describe the expression on his face was, 'Oh fuck.'

"Oaklyn." He put out his hand and started towards me.

I shook my head and backed away. Why had he kissed this woman? How was he going to have more time for them soon? What was he saying?

Why had he described the baby as 'our daughter?'

I knew, but I didn't want to know. I couldn't let myself think it, not really. Not when the reality was...

In spite of the pain, I ran off.

My sneakers thudded against the pavement in time with my heart. With every step, my bag slammed into my back, but I ignored it. The only thing that mattered right now was being anywhere but here.

"I have to go after her," Dad called out before trotting behind me. He was tall and fast, but I was running on adrenaline. Running away from what I saw. There was no way in hell I could let him catch up.

I bolted down to the end of the block, to our townhouse on the corner. The place that was always a safe sanctuary. A place of stability and love. Of two parents who adored each other.

Or so I thought.

I swung my bag down from one shoulder to grab out my key. I jammed it into the lock and shoved the front door open. Without looking to see whether or not he was behind me, I slammed it shut and took the stairs two at a time, up to my bedroom.

I threw myself and my bag inside and slammed that door too, before locking it.

That was when I realized the painkillers were downstairs. If I was going to get any, I'd have to risk going back down there.

Suddenly the pain in my stomach didn't seem so bad. Not compared to the pain in my heart.

I climbed under the covers and rolled myself into

a tight ball. As tight as I could go. As if making myself smaller would somehow ease the pain. Somehow erase what I saw. Maybe I dreamed it?

I wished I had, but I knew I hadn't. My father had a child with another woman. And he was planning to leave.

I shut out of the rest of the world, lay there and sobbed.

~

Present day

Cadence shot to her feet and gaped at me like I was out of my mind. "I wasn't born until after he left. You can't go around saying shit like that."

"Watch your language," I said, while trying not to squeeze my glass so hard it broke. "That was what happened." I didn't want to believe it either, even now.

I also shouldn't be airing all this dirty laundry in front of Nate, but he made it clear he wasn't leaving until we had this out. I let him stay, reasoning to myself that this messed up conversation might be the thing that finally put him off. He'd see I was really a basket case, and run for the mountains.

If the expression on his face was any indication, it had the opposite effect. I should have known he'd respond that way. Feel sorry for me and my sister.

"Why should I believe any of it?" She grabbed up her backpack and stormed toward the door.

"Cadence." I rose to my feet.

Nate put his hand on mine. "Let her go. She needs time to process all of this."

I glanced down at him before sinking back into my seat. I needed time to process all of it too. My head was spinning from...everything.

Up until now, I'd all but put my sister out of my mind. After Dad left, none of it seemed to matter anymore. He was out of my life. I tried not to think about him. I focused on work and moving from one city to the next before landing here, in Lowball Bay.

When I left Seattle behind, I thought I'd start a whole new chapter. Now... I was right back where I started. To further complicate things, I wasn't oblivious to the zing of electricity that passed through me at Nate's touch.

What was the level below basket case anyway?

"Are you okay?" Nate asked. His hand was still

on mine, the pad of his thumb slowly sliding back and forth across my skin.

"Just peachy," I said with a shake of my head. "When I woke up this morning, this was exactly where I hoped to end up."

"Sitting with me?" he asked, a cheeky glint in his eye.

I pulled my hand back away from his and placed it in my lap. "You must think my family is messed up. I mean, my father had a family with another woman."

I never understood why. Were my mother and I not enough for him? He was supposed to love her forever, not have a child with another woman.

Rebecca. All I knew about her was her first name.

"Who does stuff like that?"

Yeah, I knew the answer to that question. Men who could never be satisfied with one woman. Players. Men like Nate Southwell. Men I always seemed to attract for some reason. Was it because I was like my mother? Somehow we drew men like that to us? What was it about us that said 'please, screw me over?'

"An asshole," Nate said decisively. "A dick who hasn't figured out what he wants, or, I dunno, they've decided they want everything all at once. Someone who doesn't deserve you or Cadence."

"I guess so," I said, my gaze on the worn top of the table. The surface was chipped here and there, a stain from something blue on the edge near my glass.

I might be more like my father than I realized. I'd always found it hard to settle down in one place. I could be a personal trainer almost anywhere, and that's what I spent the last handful of years doing. When I was tired of a place, I moved on. It kept me from getting bored.

Or so I told myself.

"Look at me," Nate said. Then more firmly, "Oaklyn, look at me."

I slowly raised my eyes to his. He looked worried, but it was fleeting. It had to be. He'd forget about all of this soon enough. He was too busy training, traveling, playing and chasing women to be distracted for long.

What I was doing right now was humoring him, which wasn't fair to either of us.

"What your father did, it sucks. If he was here right now, I'd be tempted to punch him in the face and tell him to fuck all the way off. What he did was disgusting. To you and to your mom. But y'know, some good came out of it."

"Yeah, what's that?" I asked. Because right now, I couldn't think of a single thing.

"You and your sister," he said. "From what I saw, she's pretty awesome." He scratched at his cheek and let out a slow breath. "She's just lost both of her parents. I dunno, but right now I think she needs her big sister."

If I felt bad before, it immediately increased a hundredfold. He was right. I was here wallowing in self pity over what my father did, and hadn't even stopped to think what Cadence must be going through. Not to mention how she got here from Seattle in the first place.

I had no idea about...anything. She turned up on my doorstep and I threw a truth bomb right in the middle of her existence.

Who's the screw up here? That would be me.

"You're right," I said finally. "I've done nothing so far but make this harder for her. If I was her, I'd be halfway back to Seattle by now." Or at least on the way to the airport or bus station. Maybe the train. She was too young to drive all that way. I hoped she hadn't. She'd taken enough risks already.

"I have a feeling she hasn't gone that far," he said. He nodded towards the window.

Cadence sat on a bench across the road, her back

to us, knees drawn up to her chin. Her head was down, but it was definitely her.

"I should go to her," I said. "Thank you. You didn't have to stick around."

"Yes, I did," he said. "I wouldn't be anywhere else. Are you going to be okay?"

"Probably not, but you're late for practice." I spotted assistant coach, Valentina Ortiz in the corner of my eye, headed toward the table. One of the first female coaches in the NHL, she wouldn't pull any punches in telling him where he should be and what he should be doing right now.

He groaned.

I leaned over and patted his shoulder before pushing my chair in under the table. "Good luck."

We probably both needed some of that right now.

Chapter Four

Nate

"H EY, C OACH." I GRABBED THE HALF EMPTY juice glasses from the table to carry them back to the counter.

Valentina held a thermal cup in her hand, or I would have offered to buy her a coffee. Just to be nice. Nothing to do with wanting to bribe her so she didn't tear me a new one for being late.

"Southwell." She sipped her coffee and regarded me with dark eyes that gave away nothing.

"I was just on my way," I said, with one eye on the window as Oaklyn appeared, moving briskly toward Cadence.

If the teenager knew she was there, I couldn't tell from here. Cadence hadn't stood up and run away yet. That had to be a good sign, right? She might bolt as soon as she realized her sister was approaching, but she wasn't on a bus home already.

"Is this the reason you've been late to practice more often than not recently?" Valentina asked.

What was it with women making me wince this morning? It was starting to become a habit.

"On a scale of one to ten, how much shit am I in?" I asked. Honestly, I wasn't as worried as I let on. As soon as Zack said anything stupid, or Blake's latest prank was discovered, they'd forget about me being a couple of minutes late here or there.

"You answer my question first." Valentina waved towards the window with her coffee mug. "Are you bothering the arena staff?"

"I wouldn't say so much bothering as..." Waiting to claim what was mine? Yeah, accurate, but I couldn't say that to Valentina.

"Testing out the equipment in the staff gym. Wouldn't want any of that to be substandard." As if anything here was substandard. Not after Andi Welling took over the team. She was gradually updating everything that needed to be updated, and even planned to add a daycare to the facility.

When he heard about it, Zack suggested I belonged there, to be looked after while the adults did their thing. I'd flipped him off and ignored him for the rest of the day. Standard operating procedure when it came to him.

Valentina bought exactly zero of what I said, that much was clear in the dry glance she sent my way. But I was on a roll, so why stop now?

"Not all heroes wear capes, right Coach?"

I caught a glimpse of Oaklyn lowering herself to the seat. Near her sister, but giving her some space at the same time.

Cadence still wasn't running, but her posture was stiffer than a hockey stick.

I rubbed my chin. I should have been out there, helping them to sort things out. Or at least, trying not to make them worse.

I was a defenseman, I didn't like to feel defenceless. I also knew Oaklyn wouldn't be impressed if I blew off practice, or suggested she couldn't handle things with her sister. She was one of the most independent woman I ever met. Her exterior was tougher than steel.

I was itching to get underneath it and see the woman inside.

"You're full of shit, Southwell," Valentina told me. "Right now I'm thinking how many drills to put you through this morning. You know, to remind you why you're here. In case you forgot, it has something to do with ice hockey. A game you get paid a few bucks to play."

No doubt she knew exactly how many bucks I got paid. More than a few. And, like Oaklyn, she knew exactly how to get to me.

Since I started playing for the NHL, I'd watched the dollars roll in, and my stress about money roll out. Bringing that up was the fastest way to wipe the smile off my face.

If she was one of my teammates, I would have said it was a low blow, but I decided it was better not to bite back. Not with her. If I was honest, I wanted her to respect me as much as I respected her. She deserved that for putting up with us players. Not to mention the social media bullshit that went along with all of it.

"I don't mind doing all the drills, Coach," I told her. "Oaklyn needed a friend and I was here for her." I wasn't going to let Valentina think she had me by the balls. Only one woman could do that. Okay, two, because my mother was even more intimidating than the assistant coach, or Oaklyn.

"Is everything all right?" Valentina leaned to the side to look around me, out the window. The flicker of concern in her eyes was a rare, tiny crack in her usual stony façade.

"It will be," I said.

It wasn't my place to tell anyone what was going on with Oaklyn and Cadence. If I did, Oaklyn might literally have me by the balls, and not in a good way. I was younger than her, but I wasn't stupid.

"They'll work things out."

Valentina looked like she might go outside and see for herself, but she finally nodded and gestured towards the door. "We should get to the rink. We've already missed enough as it is. Next time, do me a favor and answer your messages. It would have saved me having to go looking for you."

I frowned at her for a moment, then patted my pockets. "Shit, where's my phone?"

Loads of the twenty-six-year-olds I knew were almost surgically attached to theirs. Me, I was always putting mine down somewhere and forgetting about it. Much to the irritation of everyone, including my mother. "I probably left it in the gym."

"I should staple that thing to your forehead," Valentina said, looking unamused.

"It might be a bit hard for me to read the screen," I pointed out.

"You'd find a way," she said. "Go on, get your phone and get to the rink before I add another fifty reps to the drills you're already doing."

"Yes, Coach," I quipped before taking a last glance towards the window and trotting away to the gym.

Now, where did I leave the damn device? When I arrived an hour or so earlier, I was thinking of Oaklyn, not my phone. That line of thought never failed to send my blood right out of my brain, straight to my cock.

"Where are you?" I caught the stares from a couple of staff who came in for an early workout. They looked like they thought I'd lost my mind. I flashed them a grin.

"Just looking for my phone," I explained. "Ah, there it is."

Right where I left it, on the weight bench, beside my T-shirt. And my hoodie, which I'd forgotten about until now.

I snatched up both, shrugged into the hoodie and pushed my phone into my pocket. Not before I caught the notifications on the screen from Valentina and Coach Lampton.

And one from Flynn Weston, center and team captain. Also the first person I saw when I finally stepped onto the ice with my skates on, stick in hand.

"Nice of you to join us, Southwell." He nodded to me. "Is everything okay?" He wasn't that much older than the rest of the team, but he assumed the role of father to all of us. Or tried to, anyway.

"Everything's dope." I returned his nod.

"Good. You know if you need to talk about anything—"

I interrupted him. "Thanks, I appreciate it."

I would have liked to confide in someone, but once again it wasn't my story to tell. It was one hell of a story though. Oaklyn's father having another family and leaving hers? The whole thing blew my mind.

Hers too, I gathered. Not to mention Cadence's. The poor kid probably felt like her whole life was torn apart. I mean, it basically was. Just like Oaklyn's was when she saw her father with newborn Cadence. That must have hurt like a bitch.

I wished I could have been there for her, but decided not to remind myself I was ten years old at the time. Too busy playing pond hockey to give a shit about much else.

That was then, this was now. I could be here for her when she needed me, and I would.

"You angling for a new nickname?" Cam North called out to me. When I gave him a funny look, he grinned. "Late Nate."

Smart ass.

"Your ability to rhyme is next level," I said sarcastically. Unfortunately, off the top of my head, I couldn't think of anything that rhymed with either Cam or North.

"You should become a poet when you retire," Zack Reed told Cam as he skated past. He looked tired for some reason, but I didn't ask why. He'd made it very clear when he joined the team that he didn't give a shit about our problems as long as we didn't give a shit about his. If that was how he wanted to play it, whatever. I wouldn't lose any sleep over it.

"Maybe I will," Cam called after Zack. He nodded toward Blake Eastwood and grinned, making me turn to look too.

It was my turn to grin.

The team's goalie was holding his arms above his head, the tips of his gloved fingers pressed together. Head tipped back, he was doing slow pirouettes on the ice while the goalie coach had a quick conversation with the head coach. Even with all of his padding on, he was graceful.

"Sometimes I think he's not all there," Cam remarked.

"Only sometimes?" I laughed. Blake was a typical goalie. Lively and weird as fuck. It came with the territory and was probably enhanced by one too many hits to the head by flying pucks.

"I could teach you to do ballet like this," Blake offered as he slowly turned. "You could be a chick magnet like me."

"I don't need to be a chick magnet," Cam said smugly, as if anyone here needed reminding he was dating Andi.

"I'm already a chick magnet," I said. Unless you counted the one chick I actually wanted to magnetize.

Almost as one, we turned to look at Flynn.

He looked back at us, a frown visible under his visor. "I'm not taking up ballet."

"Too girly for you?" Zack offered. "No, wait, not girly enough." He actually looked impressed with his own dig. Of course he would, someone had to be. The rest of us weren't.

"You say girly like it's a bad thing," Valentina said from where she stood beside the boards. She looked less than amused. Cadence could learn a thing or two from her.

Flynn gave her a quick glance and in a tight voice said, "Let's get back to it."

If I didn't know better, I'd think he didn't like her for some reason. Her appointment as assistant coach certainly raised some eyebrows across all sides of the NHL.

Eyebrows I tended to ignore. An excellent coach was an excellent coach as far as I was concerned. Whatever Flynn's problem was, I wasn't going to make it mine either. He'd get over it.

Zack, looking deflated and even a little humbled, muttered something that actually sounded like, "Sorry, Coach," before skating to the other side of the rink and focusing on drills. Or pretending to.

I must have misheard, because I'd never heard him apologize for anything in the couple of years we'd been playing together. I got it though. If anyone was going to intimidate him, it would be Valentina. She probably knew a way to kick so her foot went straight past the cup to score a direct hit on our balls.

"Girly is a good thing, Coach," Blake said. He'd stopped doing pirouettes and was standing in front of the goal with his legs apart, attention now more or less focused on the goalie coach. "But if anyone thinks ballet is girly, they should try it sometime. It's harder than this." He threw himself to the side to stop the puck with his catcher.

"Maybe I should sign all of you up for classes," Coach Lampton said dryly. "I hear it's good exercise." He waved his hand at us. "Enough distractions. Turn and burn, boys and girls. Turn and burn."

Stick in hand, I ran across the ice, but the distraction wouldn't let up until I knew what Oaklyn was doing, and if she was okay.

Chapter Five

Oaklyn

THE WINTER BREEZE CAME STRAIGHT OFF THE ocean a couple of hundred feet away, ruffling my hair and making me shiver.

I wrapped my arms around myself and slowly approached Cadence. She didn't look up as I sat beside her. Her forehead was pressed against her knees. Her shoulders rose and fell evenly as she inhaled and exhaled.

"I could have been more diplomatic," I said.

"No shit." Her voice was muffled. "How would you feel?" She lifted her face and looked over at me. Her eyes were red, but dry.

"Hurt," I said. "Devastated. Probably like going into Doughballs, buying a whole chocolate cake and eating all of it on this bench."

She looked at me like I was out of my mind, or flat out lying to her. "Have you ever done that? Eaten a whole cake by yourself, I mean."

"More times than I'd like to admit," I said. "I regret it afterward, but in the moment," I shrugged one shoulder, "it's chocolate cake, y'know?"

"Yeah." She turned away and pressed her head against her legs again. "Was that true? What you said about me being born before your father left?"

I thought about telling her it wasn't, and that I exaggerated, but I wouldn't lie to her. She'd been through enough already.

"It's true," I said softly. "Why did you say he should have stayed with me and my mom?" I decided it was safe to scoot over a little closer to her.

"Because he was never there," she said after a moment of painful hesitation. "I mean, he was there physically, but he didn't seem to give a shit, y'know? I guess I know why. It's my fault. If I wasn't born, he could have stayed with you and your mom. You must hate my guts."

"I don't hate you," I said honestly. I'd spent the last sixteen years resenting her existence and wondering what would have happened if she was never born. But in the end, it was my father I placed the blame on. He was the one who cheated on my mother. He was the one who got another woman pregnant. He was the one who knew what I knew for days before he told my mother.

I always wondered if he'd hoped I'd tell her for him, to save him doing his own dirty work. Was he that much of a coward? The fact he eventually admitted what he did didn't make up for his many shortcomings. It didn't stop my mother's heart from being shattered.

She looked back up again, still skeptical. "I'd hate me."

"Do you hate me?" I asked.

Her brows knitted. They looked like someone had professionally shaped them, but they'd grown out a little. Her nails were the same. She looked like a vulnerable, young, grieving fashionista.

"Why would I hate you?" she asked.

"Because I told you the truth," I said.

"They should have done that," she said fiercely. "Unless they were too ashamed to admit it. They always seemed so... I don't know. Like they were too busy for each other too."

I wanted to put my arm around her and comfort her, but I sensed she wasn't ready for that yet. Honestly, I wasn't much of a hugger myself.

"I'm sorry you had to go through that," I said

sincerely. "It sounds to me like our father did a good job of making everyone miserable, including himself."

"Good," she said, in that unapologetic way sixteen-year-olds had. "He didn't care about me anyway."

"I don't think that's true," I said. The last person in the world I wanted to defend was him, but I wasn't going to let her continue with this line of thought. Nothing good would come of it. "He and your mother both loved you a lot. They would have done anything for you."

"Then why didn't they tell me about you?" she asked. "It wasn't until both of them were dead that social services mentioned I had a sister."

"Social services got involved?" Now I was the one frowning.

Her eyes glazed. She shrugged and looked away, towards the bakery. "I don't have any other family. My grandparents are gone. No aunts or uncles. You're the only one I have left."

I felt like the breath was knocked right out of my lungs. She was right. Our father had no siblings, and his parents passed away a handful of years ago.

"So you came and found me," I said softly. "How did you find me?"

"Google," she said. "My foster parents were at work, so I caught a bus over." She could have been talking about the next town over, not the other side of the country.

"Wait a moment." Now my head was spinning. "You ran away from your foster home and came all the way here, from Seattle, by yourself? And they have no idea where you are?"

"I'm not going back," she said quickly and with a stubborn tilt to her chin. "I'm sixteen, I should be able to take care of myself. Or decide where I live."

It took my brain a few moments to catch up to that statement. "You want to live with me? I don't think it's that simple."

"You don't want me?" She sounded hurt, but more than that, this seemed like a challenge.

"I'm not sure why you'd want to live with me," I admitted. "I don't stay anywhere for very long."

"You're all I have," she whispered.

My gut clenched. What did I know about taking care of a teenager? Especially one as independent as Cadence.

"We have to contact social services," I started.

"I'm not going back," she said again. "They don't care about me. They think I'm a smart mouthed brat. They'd be better off without me."

"I wonder what gave them that impression," I said dryly. She certainly did have a smart mouth on her. I couldn't fault her for that. I had one myself at times. I certainly never let up on Nate.

She grinned.

I rolled my eyes. "Talking to social services is not negotiable. For one thing, they have to know where you are. They probably lodged a missing persons report by now and are searching for you. I don't know, but I think wasting police resources might be illegal or something." If nothing else, we could put her foster parents' minds at ease.

"In the meantime, I guess you can stay with me and Gran." I wasn't sure what Gran was going to think about that, but I'd deal with it when the time came.

"Is Gran—" Her expression was tentative now.

"My mother's mother, yeah," I said. "She's very... Eccentric." That was an understatement. Cadence would see for herself soon enough.

"What about that hockey player guy?" Cadence asked. "Nate Southpark?"

I snorted a laugh. "Southwell. What about him?" I could see where this was going before she got there, but I decided to humor her.

"Is he your boyfriend?" she teased. Her eyes

widened. "Or your husband? You're old, you're probably married." Her brows dipped. "You're not married, but cheating with him, are you?"

Where did I even start with all of that?

I counted the points on my fingers. "First of all, I'm thirty-one, which is not old." I ignored the smirk on her face and counted the second point. "Nate is not my boyfriend and I'm not married."

"He likes you," she said. "He was worried that you were upset when I turned up. He seems nice. I think you should go for it."

"Nate is a friend, nothing more," I said firmly.

"He wants more." She gave me a sly sideways grin.

"You can't always get what you want," I said. Pointedly, because she may not be able to live with me. She could be removed and forced to return to her foster parents in Seattle. That might be for the best. I was so busy, I wasn't sure if I had time to be physically present for her, much less a parent figure.

She pouted. "Fine, we'll find you someone else then. But I think you should give him a chance."

"I don't want someone else," I said more curt than I intended. I closed my eyes for a couple of moments and shook my head. "I'm sorry. I'm just used to being single. It's comfortable. I'm happy to stay that way."

"That sounds like an old pair of sneakers," she said. "Comfortable until the soles fall off."

"That's very poetic," I told her. "I also get attached to comfortable pairs of sneakers."

"I'm shocked," she said sarcastically. "I bet you wear them until they die." She leaned over and looked down at mine. "Suspicion confirmed."

I raised a foot to look critically at my sneaker. "There's a year or two left in these yet."

Okay, they were getting worn around the edges and they weren't new when I bought them either. The only things I bought new were underwear and socks. Buying vintage clothes was good for the planet, and I didn't much care about style. Why bother when you spend most of your time in lycra?

"They were old a year or two ago," Cadence said. "But if that's your thing, I guess I can roll with it."

"I'm glad my sneakers don't have you back on the first bus back to Seattle." I eyed her, still surprised by the strong family resemblance. We both looked eerily like our father.

"It would take more than sneakers for me to run away again," she said. "I'm not that shallow. You do you."

"I'm starting to think I don't get to call myself the cool older sister," I said, with no regret at all. She gave me a look which made me sigh. "Let me guess, no one over the age of twenty could be cool."

"Twenty-six is about the upper limit," she agreed.

Nate's age. Of course he was cooler than me. That was another reason why we wouldn't work together. I'd embarrass him with my vintage sneakers and quirky style. If he even stuck around long enough to be embarrassed. Which he wouldn't, so the point was moot in the end.

"I'm going to tell you something that may devastate you," I said in a tone that suggested I was not going to say anything truly bad. "Some day, you'll be thirty too."

She stuck out her tongue in disgust. "Yeah, but by then thirty will be the new sixteen. So, by definition, I'll be cool. Can we stop saying cool so much?"

"Skibbidi." I nodded.

She groaned. "No one says that anymore! And don't suggest fetch. I've seen that movie too."

"Rad," I said instead.

I had to admit I was enjoying myself. I wasn't sure if I was any kind of role model for a kid like her, but I liked her. She reminded me of myself at that age. Full of sass. Right before my father pulled the rug out from under my feet.

"You are the cringiest big sister ever," Cadence declared. She leaned over to pat my hand. "But it's okay, we can work on you."

"Maybe I like being cringey," I offered.

"Only a cringey person would say that," she pointed out.

"I think that's the point," I said with a playful frown. I sighed and glanced down at my watch. "I have to get back to work. I'm guessing this is where you tell me you aren't staying anywhere."

"I came straight here from the bus," she said. "Maybe I could help you. I know a thing or two about gym equipment. Before Mom and Dad died, I was a gymnast. Not like Olympic level or anything, but I was pretty good. And I know my way around a yoga mat."

"I guess you could stick around for the day," I said, hoping like hell it wasn't against some sort of health and safety regulation. I was sure Andi would understand if I explained it to her. "Only for today though. You should really be in school."

She grimaced. "I should have told you I was eighteen." Her eyes widened as she realized what she said. Our father would have kept her hidden for two years before anyone found out. Or he would have left my mother sooner.

"I wouldn't have bought it," I said, as if I didn't pick up on the implications. "You look sixteen."

What she looked now was relieved. For a moment, she seemed convinced I'd drag her back to the bus station and put on the first bus to anywhere. Even if she couldn't live with me, I wouldn't do that to her. I'd make sure she was settled, whatever it took.

Although, the fact I only planned to stay in the city for six months lingered in the back of my mind.

Chapter Six

Nate

I LEANED AGAINST THE DOOR FRAME AND watched Oaklyn. She was watching Cadence, who was on the floor doing yoga with Ursula, the receptionist. The pink haired woman was following the teenager's movements, trying to stretch in the same way.

Oaklyn must have noticed me watching, because she turned to make a face at me.

I took that as my cue to saunter into the room, hands in my pockets.

"Looks like you sorted things out."

Oaklyn sighed. "You could say that."

"You wouldn't say that?" I cocked my head at her.

She looked as worried as she had when Cadence

ran out of the café. Like the weight of the world rested on her shoulders and she wasn't going to hand it off to anyone else. Whether she liked it or not, I was going to spot her. Standing this close to her, I wanted to do a lot of other things too. Nothing suitable for the current audience. Although, since Cadence was occupied—

She put a hand on my arm, just above my elbow, sending a jolt of heat straight to my groin. Yeah, even through the thick, plush fabric of my hoodie. What can I say, I had it bad.

When she drew me off to the side of the room, I followed like a faithful puppy. One who very much wanted to do it doggy style with her. And I would, when the time was right.

Soon, I told myself. I wanted to lose myself deep inside her, feel her muscles tighten around me as she screamed my name and came. That was in my top two sounds I needed, wanted to hear, her letting go while I gave her orgasm after orgasm, until she was exhausted and satisfied. Number two was hearing her come again.

"She ran away from her foster parents," Oaklyn whispered, bringing me back to the present. "I've contacted social services, but they can't send anyone out for the next couple of days at least. They're slammed this time of year. And apparently..." She winced. "A sixteen-year-old isn't the top priority."

"Poor kid," I whispered back. I glanced at Cadence, but she was trying to show Ursula a move the receptionist apparently couldn't grasp.

Cadence wasn't holding back in showing her frustration either. I wondered if she realized how much like her sister she was. How deep did that go? Right now, they were practically strangers.

"She's going to stay with me for a while, but I'm not sure if that's a good idea," Oaklyn was saying.

I turned back to her. I liked that she was comfortable enough to confide in me like this. Maybe she was just desperate to have another adult to talk to. Yes, I am an actual adult, in spite of what my teammates might say. Ask my mother, she'll tell you.

"Why not?" I asked. "It'll give you a chance to get to know each other. You want that, right?" If my sister turned up out of the blue, I'd want to get to know her. Especially if she ran away to find me.

"Yes?" Oaklyn's brow dipped adorably. "She's my sister, but it's not that simple."

"It seems simple to me," I said. "She has nowhere to go and she's your sister. What else is there to think about?"

"I worry I'd be a bad influence on her," Oaklyn

said. "What if I say the wrong thing, or do something stupid?" She almost looked like she was in physical pain from the idea of screwing up.

Messing up her own life, that was one thing, but throw a kid into the mix? This was a puck she didn't see coming until it struck her. She couldn't have caught or deflected it, even if she tried. Cadence's appearance had taken her completely by surprise. Honestly, it was a credit to her that she hadn't lost her shit completely. I wasn't sure if I'd be so calm if I was in her shoes.

"I hate to admit this, but I do stupid shit all the time," I said. "If I worried about it, I'd never do anything again. How boring would that be?"

"I don't think you could ever be boring," she said.

"Yeah, well." I rubbed a hand over the back of my neck. "That's true." I ducked to the side slightly when I thought she might sock me for my lack of modesty.

"I shouldn't even be having this conversation with you," she said, looking exasperated. "I should just—" She started to turn away.

"Stop," I said, my tone firm, insisting on obedience.

She stopped and turned back to me, her eyes wide. Dark and getting darker. So that's how it was? I could work with this. My cock was going to be hard as hell if we kept on like this, but it was progress.

I placed my hands on her shoulders, my fingers gripping, holding her there. "Talk to me. What's really got you bothered?"

She tried to avert her gaze, but I squeezed her shoulders more firmly.

"She needs a parent," Oaklyn said finally. "I don't know if I can be what she needs me to be. Or if I'll even be allowed to. There are processes with things like this, aren't there? Social services, courts, who knows what else."

"Then we go through those processes," I said as if nothing was simpler. "If both of you decide you can't live together, maybe they can find somewhere close. Somewhere in Lowball Bay where she can get what she needs. Ursula might adopt her." I was half joking, but they did seem to be getting along relatively well.

"I can't begin to tell you what's wrong with that," Oaklyn said. When I gave her a questioning look, she added, "I mean it. I can't begin to tell you if it's wrong or right. Crazy or brilliant. I have absolutely no idea. My only experience with sixteen-year-olds was being one once. And going to school with them. A very, very long time ago."

I wanted to shake her for saying that. "It was *not* that long ago."

I remembered being sixteen and it wasn't pretty. Now I thought about it, her reluctance made sense. I was wild at that age. Obsessed with hockey, and ambitious as hell. Determined to get out of Highball Creek by any means necessary. I'd wanted to become an engineer, but we couldn't afford college, so I threw everything I had into my sport. It was something I could do. Something I was good at. Better than good. It changed my life and I'd never looked back. Until now.

Now, I wondered what sixteen-year-old Nate would think of me and where I was. I decided he'd be pretty happy, but it was a long road to get here.

"It feels like a lifetime right now," she said wearily. "I thought I put all of this behind me but here it is, right in my face."

I wanted to kiss her. To take her mind off everything. I dropped my gaze from her beautiful blue eyes to her plush lips.

She swallowed audibly. She must have seen where I was looking and what I was thinking. She moistened her lips with her tongue.

I wanted nothing more right now than to taste her mouth. To hear her moan. To touch and caress her until she finally understood her body was mine and so was she.

Right beside us, Cadence cleared her throat. I hadn't seen her coming, but Oaklyn's response was more violent than mine. She started before jumping back, away from me.

"I, shoot— I mean..." Her face turned pink. "Nothing was happening."

Cadence hummed in the back of her throat. "Sure." She gave me the side eye before turning to her sister. "You told me to tell you when Ursula was finished. I guess you didn't notice she'd gone."

Oaklyn looked around, clearly embarrassed to find only the three of us were left in the gym.

I wasn't embarrassed. Not at all. This just proved she was into me as much as I was into her. She just needed to admit it.

"Right." Oaklyn shook her head slowly to clear it. "Okay, good. Great." She really was distracted by me. It was fucking adorable.

"Dinner," I said. "We all need to eat." It was a little early, but I'd be on the road for the next few days, so I wanted to make the most of it while I was here in Lowball Bay.

"I should get Cadence to my place and settle her in," Oaklyn said.

"I'll get something for all of us and bring it over then," I said.

I wasn't going to let her go through this alone. I meant what I said when I told her we'd go through the process. Whatever it took to get Cadence settled, I was along for the ride. Innuendo completely intended.

"Gran will be wanting something too," Oaklyn started to protest.

"Then I'll bring enough for Gran," I said easily. "Cadence, what's your favorite food?"

Was it sneaky to get her on side, knowing Oaklyn couldn't say no once Cadence agreed to let me get dinner? Maybe. Did I give a shit? Hell to the no. If it meant spending more time with Oaklyn, then I'd do it. Shamelessly.

Cadence smirked at me, seeing right through me. She rolled her eyes and I grinned back. "I like clam chowder." She lifted her chin like there was no way I'd be able to find that anywhere in Lowball Bay.

"Clam chowder it is," I said. "Oaklyn?"

"I'm good with whatever," she said.

I doubted that. She had her favorite food, like everyone else. but she didn't want to be a hassle. Not that she could possibly be one. Not to me. If she wanted a pail full of Rainier cherries, I'd get her one.

If she wasn't going to give me anything else, then I'd figure something out. This might be a test of some kind, one I was determined to pass. I'd find something for her that she'd love. I already had a couple of ideas brewing in the back of my mind.

"Chowder and whatever, coming up." I grinned. I gave Oaklyn an expectant look, which she finally noticed when she was done making a face at my dumb joke. "I need your address."

She looked at me like somehow I contrived all of this just to get my foot in the door of her place. I was good, but even I couldn't make the universe move like that. I had no idea her sister would turn up today, or even that she had one. Or a Gran, for that matter.

Her life was a closed book, but I was going to peel the cover back, until it was wide open. Then I was going to explore, page by page. I'd read every single word until I knew everything about her.

Then I'd spend the rest of my life learning more.

Chapter Seven

Oaklyn

Cadence spent the whole drive looking out the window. I asked her a couple of questions, which she responded to with single word answers. After the third time, I gave up and drove in silence. No doubt she had a lot on her mind. I knew I did. Too many thoughts were jumbled in my brain to tease out just one to obsess over. Everything was as complicated as everything else.

I pulled into the driveway of Gran's house and turned off the engine. My old rust bucket shuddered and fell silent. Like my sneakers, it was far from new, and probably just as destined for the trash. Also like my sneakers, I couldn't bear to get rid of my vintage vehicle. As long as she ran, then she'd do me fine.

"This is where you live?" Cadence climbed out

of the car and opened the back door to reach in for her backpack.

I thought better of making a joke about dropping her off at some stranger's house and grabbed my own bag out of the back of the car.

"Yeah, this is my Gran's house. I'm staying here to help take care of her while she recovers from a broken wrist." According to her, she fell while skateboarding. Not much held her back, not even a fracture. If I was honest. I was the one who insisted on staying with her, even as she said she didn't need any help. The truth was, I needed somewhere to stay and I didn't like the idea of her living alone.

I ignored the fact she'd be living alone again when I moved on.

"It's older than your shoes," Cadence remarked.

"Most houses are older than my shoes," I said. I didn't bother to lock my car. I dropped the keys into my bag and headed up to the front door of the mid-century modern bungalow. The front door was hidden from the street by a wall of breeze blocks. The door itself was bright orange.

I pushed the door open and we stepped back into the nineteen seventies. Gran had the place decorated to fit the era, so everything was orange, brown and yellow. Furniture in shapes that can only be described as groovy.

"All the other houses look newer." Cadence looked around like she was in a museum.

"All the other houses are newer," I said. "This was one of the first houses in Lowball Bay. Everything else was built up around it. Developers have been trying to get their hands on the place for years." The block itself was so big it could accommodate an apartment building.

"Why not sell to them then?" Cadence said.

"Because they're all a bunch of motherfucking leeches," Gran said from the kitchen. "Who the hell is that?"

I groaned inwardly. My grandmother had a mouth on her like... Like a professional hockey player. She also had no filter.

"There's someone you should meet." I placed my bag and phone down on the console table near the door and beckoned Cadence over to the kitchen doorway.

Gran stood at the bright orange countertop, stirring a spoon through a cup of black coffee. Today she was dressed in a bright pink, bulky knit sweater over camo pants and chunky boots. She wore a purple bucket hat over her buzz cut hair. Massive earrings peeked out from under the brim. One was shaped like a bright yellow duck, the other like a black cat.

She pulled the spoon out of the coffee and sucked on it loudly before tossing it into the sink. One day, I'd talk her into getting a dishwasher.

"Cadence, this is Henrietta Gladys Henstridge, my grandmother."

"Everyone calls me Henri, or Gran," Gran said. She peered at Cadence. "Do I know you?"

Cadence was staring at her with a combination of confusion and awe. That quickly changed to a mask of teenage disinterest, which I began to realize was a shield against the world.

"You'd remember me if we met before," Cadence said.

Gran cackled. "That's one hell of an assumption. People my age don't always remember everything, and some people aren't that memorable." That was a challenge if I ever saw one.

"Gran, Cadence is—"

"Awesome," Cadence finished for me.

Gran cackled again. "You've got some balls, kid. She, he, they/them?"

"She/her," Cadence said. "You?"

This conversation was not going as I expected it to, but at least they didn't hate each other. Yet.

"Same, same," Gran said. "So, who the fuck are you?"

"Gran, watch your mouth," I scolded. "She's sixteen."

"You'd think she's never heard 'fuck' before?" Gran asked. "Hell, she's probably said it more times than I have. Besides, words like that are good for you. They help you to get out all your inner frustration." She waved a finger at me. "It wouldn't hurt you to drop a few F-bombs around here and there. I don't know what your mother taught you, but holding back shit like that isn't good for your nervous system."

I closed my eyes for a few moments. I had a feeling she'd have a few more expletives to drop before the night was over.

"Gran, Cadence is my half-sister," I said finally. "Dad's other baby."

"That cheating, motherfucking fuckface," Gran declared. "Has he dumped her on you? The useless piece of shit."

A drawn out silence was ended with quiet words from Cadence.

"He's dead. My mother too."

I'd never seen Gran dumbstruck, but she was now.

Until she perked up and said, "Hot diggity

damn. It's about time he went to hel—" She couldn't finish with my hand clamped over her mouth.

"Cadence doesn't need you to be happy that he's gone," I said firmly. "She's been through a lot in the last..." I glanced at her. "How long has it been?"

"Six months," she said. "And three days. Or is it four?" She shrugged indifferently.

My hand dropped from Gran's mouth. My father had been dead for six months and I had no idea? I supposed the only person who would reach out about it was Cadence, and she had. More or less.

I gave Gran the side eye before she decided to say anything else bad about him. "Cadence needs somewhere to stay. I told her she could stay here for a while. We could get her enrolled in Lowball Bay High in the morning."

Gran grunted and rubbed her wrist. The cast was removed a couple of weeks ago. I was mindful of the fact she didn't need me anymore, but I couldn't bring myself to think about looking for somewhere else to live. If I did that, staying in the city might start to feel permanent. The moment that happened, I'd want to leave. Like I always did when I got comfortable anywhere.

"How long?" Gran asked. She reached for her

coffee and took a sip. Smacked her lips together in appreciation.

"As long as it takes," I said. "She won't cause any trouble." I gave Cadence a meaningful look.

"I've never met a teenager who didn't cause any trouble," Gran said. "That's how they learn. Shame your mother wasn't so good at learning."

"She learned eventually," I said. To Cadence I said, "Mom remarried a couple of years ago. He's nice."

"Anyone who isn't a cheating prick is an improvement over your father," Gran said. "Fine, the kid can stay for a while. But no weed. And by that, I mean, no smoking inside the house, and without me. You bring that shit in here, you better be ready to share it."

"Gran," I scolded. "No weed. She's underage."

"Don't be such a stick in the mud," she scolded back. "When was the last time you had any fun, Oaklyn Jane Walsh? I take that back, you're not a stick in the mud. You've got a stick up your ass, that's what. You don't have a stick up your ass, do you kid?"

"No stick," Cadence said. "I don't like weed anyway. The one time I tried it, it made me sick."

"I bet it wasn't good quality weed," Gran said. "You need the good stuff. If you try—"

I clapped my hand to my forehead. What the heck was I thinking bringing my sister here? My grandmother might be the worst influence a teenager could have. Right now, I wasn't sure which of them would lead the other astray. I could go to work tomorrow and come back to a house that was completely trashed and stinking of weed smoke. The pair of them might turn the place into a drug den, for all I knew.

Gran chuckled. "You always were too easy to bait, Oaklyn. I haven't had a joint in a couple of years. I stick to gummies these days."

"Well, that's a relief," I said sarcastically, while Cadence looked disappointed.

Gran whispered loudly. "Someday we'll get her to loosen up, right, kid?"

Cadence grinned.

I decided a change of subject might be in the cards right about now. "I have a friend coming over soon. He's bringing us dinner."

"Oaklyn has a boyfriend," Cadence said.

"He's not my boyfriend," I protested. "Nate is just a friend."

Gran's eyes lit up. "Nate Southwell? If you don't want him, I can teach him a thing or two. Back in my day I was considered quite the— Female equivalent of a stud muffin? Whatever it is, that's what I was." She pulled off her bucket hat to scratch the top of her head before replacing it. "Now I think about it, I still am. Robert from my guitar classes has had his eye on me for a while now. He's in his forties, but I know that look. When you have it bad, you have it bad. It's only a matter of time before we consummate that."

Cadence grimaced. "Ewww, old people sex.

I grimaced. "Ewww, my grandmother sex."

"Ewww, jealousy," Gran said with a gleeful smile. "It's not my fault if I can get laid and Oaklyn can't."

"There's a difference between can't and don't want to," I said.

I didn't doubt for a moment that if I gave Nate the word, he'd happily take me to bed. Or couch. Or the back of a car. Or the weight bench in the gym. Or wherever. Now my lady parts were thinking of him and how it would feel to have him touch me. To slide inside me. To have him lie over me while he thrust slowly.

I shoved the mental image away with as much force as I could manage. It took some doing. The picture was enticing. Way too enticing, if I was honest. I couldn't let him get under my skin any deeper. For both our sakes. Okay, mostly mine. He'd forget about me quickly enough.

Maybe I should think about moving on sooner.

"Yeah, one I believe, the other I don't," Gran said. "I guess we can get Cadence settled into the spare room. It's small, but it'll do for now."

"Thanks," Cadence said in a small voice.

"Of course," I said. "You're family."

Gran waved for Cadence to proceed her out of the kitchen, but before they stepped away, she gave me a look to remind me that Cadence wasn't her family. Even if she liked the girl, she was still her father's daughter and my grandmother hated him with the passion of a thousand suns. After what he did to her daughter, I could hardly blame her.

That was just another complication in a long line of complications. It felt to me like they were piling on top of each other, one by one. If that continued, they'd rival the Ballpark Tower, the needle-like structure that dominated the city skyline. It reminded me of the Space Needle in Seattle, but taller, and newer.

Right on cue came another complication, this one accompanied by the sound of a vigorous knock on the door. "I come bearing food!"

I ignored the way my heart skipped a beat and

my pulse raced a little faster, and stepped over to open the door.

Chapter Eight

Nate

"HOW'S THE CHOWDER?"

Cadence was eating as though she hadn't eaten in days, until I asked that. She slowed down, playing it cool before shrugging one shoulder. "It's okay."

I exchanged glances with Oaklyn and smiled. "Is your 'whatever' okay too?"

"Best 'whatever' I ever had," she said. "I like lobster rolls."

I bit into mine, hoping not to look too relieved. I was trying to play it cool in front of Gran and Cadence. Okay, mostly in front of Oaklyn.

It had been a while since I had anything like a family meal. Something about this felt right, in spite of the tension that still crackled through the air. No one was entirely comfortable with the situation, that much was subtly obvious. As in, not right in your face, but clear enough.

"Fish Balls makes the best lobster rolls and clam chowder in the city," I said. "In summer, it's so popular they sell out if you don't get there fast enough."

"You ain't lying," Gran said. "I've been there when there was a line around the block. By the time I got there, all they had left was crumbs and fries. Luckily they also do the best fries in the city." She picked up one and bit into it.

"I think that's her way of saying thank you for bringing dinner," Oaklyn said. "We appreciate it. Right, Cadence?"

Cadence shrugged and dipped a fry into her chowder before tossing it into her mouth. "Sure."

"It's okay, you don't need to tell me how awesome I am," I said. "I already know, and you're welcome. The real question is, when are you going to admit the clam chowder is better than anything you had back home?"

Cadence eyed me over her spoon. "Clam chowder is clam chowder."

"I think she likes it," Oaklyn said. "It certainly stands up to what they have back east."

I picked up a fry and pointed it at her. "This is better and you know it. I also know I'm going to have to do an extra workout tomorrow to work off all of this." Meaning of course I'd get to spend more time with Oaklyn.

"Me too," she said, patting her flat stomach. She'd changed out of her lycra and into a pair of bell bottom jeans and a faded floral peasant blouse. Over the top of that, she wore a pale green cardigan with a small hole in the shoulder. She was even more adorable in the vintage clothes. She fit in with the decor of Gran's house.

I suspected if I told her that, she'd deck me.

"So, you play hockey, hmmm?" Gran asked.

"I've been known to dabble," I said modestly, ignoring Oaklyn's snort of disbelief.

"Are you any good?" Gran asked.

"Gran, you know he plays professionally," Oaklyn said.

"I know, but I want to hear it from him." Gran nodded toward me.

"I can hold my own out on the ice," I said. "I'd like to think I don't suck at it."

"What do you suck at?" Gran asked.

Oaklyn pressed the tips of her fingers to her forehead and shook her head. Evidently she found her grandmother's inquisition embarrassing.

"I've never been very good at cooking," I admitted. "But where I excel in the kitchen is washing and drying dishes. If that was a sport, I'd go pro there too."

It was Cadence's turn to snort. "Professional dishwashing?"

I grinned. "Why not? Let's not stop there. *Olympic* dishwashing. I'd be a shoe-in for a gold medal."

The look she gave me suggested she was thinking I was a shoe-in for craziest person in the house right now. Which, from what I've seen of Gran, was saying something.

"Maybe you can display those skills after dinner," Oaklyn suggested.

"I'll get the sheets of paper," Gran said. When we all turned to look at her questioningly, she explained, "So we can write the scores on them. I'll tell you now, boyo, you're gonna have to make those dishes clean as fuck before I give you anything above an eight."

"I'm not related to her, am I?" Cadence asked Oaklyn.

"No, you're not," Oaklyn assured her. "Sometimes I wonder if I am."

Gran chortled loudly. "I've wondered the same thing. But now you have this hot boyfriend of yours, maybe you'll lighten up and be more like me."

"He's not my boyfriend," Oaklyn said.

"Boyfriend, lover, whatever." Gran waved a hand in the air dismissively. "We don't have to label everything, including the description for the person we're fucking."

Oaklyn turned a fascinating shade of pink. "Gran! We're not..." She placed her whole hand over her eyes and shook her head.

"Yet," Cadence said.

"Not you too," Oaklyn said, her eyes still covered. "Nate and I are just friends, right Nate?"

I waited until she parted her fingers to peer at me before I bit into my lobster roll. We weren't fucking, but Cadence was right, it was only a matter of time. Now was not the moment to call that fact out. The last thing I wanted to do was piss Oaklyn off, especially in front of her grandmother and sister. Her not talking to me would make claiming her more difficult.

"Is he going to be moving in here next?" Gran asked.

"I should get you season tickets to our home games," I told her. "The team would love you. Maybe we could convince Andi to put Cece, the mascot, out to pasture and replace her with you." Not that the red sea dragon wasn't cute, but Gran would get the crowd going like crazy. I bet she could whip them into a frenzy without raising a sweat.

"Can you put a sea dragon out to pasture?" Cadence asked.

"In this case, yes," I said. "Don't suggest throwing her out to sea if Blake Eastwood is around. He'd take you literally."

That had her looking curious. "How?"

I dipped a fry into my creamy chowder and bit into it before responding. "One of two ways comes to mind. The first involves throwing the mascot into the sea, maybe from a boat? The other involves stealing the mascot costume and jumping off the top of the rollercoaster or the Ferris wheel at the pier." I could easily imagine the goalie doing both of those things. And the team having to replace the costume in between each. No, it was better if he didn't get that idea.

"No," Oaklyn said to Gran.

"I didn't say a word," Gran protested, a smile on the corners of her mouth.

"You don't have to say anything, I know what you're thinking. You're not jumping off the rollercoaster into the ocean. Especially not wearing a heavy mascot costume." Oaklyn gave her a firm look, like she was the adult in the room.

"Think of the glory." Gran tilted her head back and gazed up at the ceiling, a dreamy look in her eyes.

"Think of how you might drown," Oaklyn said.

Gran waved a hand at me. "Nate will make sure I don't drown. Won't you, Nate?"

"Nate isn't going anywhere near a stunt like that," Oaklyn said. "Right, Nate?" Her molars were pressed together.

"I don't want to encourage that behavior," I started slowly. *Depending on the circumstances.* "But if you're there, making sure nothing happens to Gran, I'd have to be there to make sure you're okay."

Suggesting a crazy stunt like that to Blake seemed more and more viable, if only to prevent Gran from doing it herself. He had a slightly better chance of surviving than Oaklyn's grandmother would.

On the other hand, I could picture the expression on the face of Alice North, the team's social media/PR goddess. Younger sister of Cam North, she already had to put out at least a dozen, non-literal, fires Blake lit. Several times, she'd managed to talk him down from doing something she'd have to fix later. This would definitely get him, and me, on her shit list.

Since she was exactly one of the people it was best to stay on the good side of, I'd keep my mouth shut. I wouldn't be held responsible if he thought of it himself. He was very creative at getting himself into trouble.

"I'd be there to take pictures and post them on social media," Cadence said helpfully. "I'd bet they'd go viral in about half an hour." She seemed to like the idea.

"See? It's a family thing now," Gran said. "Although, it's a bit cold this time of year. We can wait until spring." She looked thoughtful, like she was seriously considering setting a date for it here and now. And trying to work out a way to get her hands on a mascot costume. If she was thinking about asking me, I might have a conflict of interest in that Oaklyn would probably throttle me if I helped.

Oaklyn pressed her lips together so hard they turned white. "Can I convince you to bungee jump instead? Please? You've only just got your cast off."

"Fuck yeah!" Gran was almost jumping up and

down in her chair with excitement. "One hundred percent you can talk into bungee jumping. It's been at least a year or two since I did it. Or went skydiving, for that matter."

"I wish my grandmother was as cool as you." I sighed. "Mine likes to stay at home and bake pies." Really good pies. Pies that won the blue ribbon at the state fair every year. But they weren't as exciting as jumping out of a plane and hoping like hell your parachute opened the way it was supposed to. Unless you're really, really hungry. In which case, I guessed they were that exciting.

Oaklyn muttered something that sounded like, "Do you want to swap?"

"At least you have a grandmother," Cadence said softly.

That brought the mood down faster than the final horn when the team was on the wrong side of a shutout. No one wanted to lose, and losing like that sucked hairy donkey balls. Especially when we didn't play well and only had ourselves to blame for being creamed.

"Cadence, I'm sorry, I know you've been through a lot," Oaklyn said. "We'll get things sorted out, okay?" She started to reach over to her sister.

"Can I be excused?" Cadence pushed her chair

back, the feet scraping on the hardwood floors that looked original to the house. Her mouth was turned down the sides, blue eyes looking lost and every bit as young and vulnerable as she really was.

She could put on the attitude, but at the end of the day she was a kid. One who was still grieving and trying to figure things out. Trying to find her place in the world. Hoping like hell there was one for her.

"Of course." Oaklyn sat back and placed her hands in her lap like she'd been struck. As if somehow she'd overstepped and been slapped back down.

"You must be tired after—" Oaklyn cut her words off with a click of her teeth when Cadence stalked away, swallowed by the shadows at the other end of the house.

"She's probably exhausted and still trying to wrap her head around being here," I said. "She'll be okay." I wanted to reach for Oaklyn and comfort her. Tell her it was okay to try to make her sister feel better. And that it was okay for Cadence to need some space.

"I hope so," Oaklyn said, not so sure. She looked as though she'd retreated behind a wall of steel, her emotions collected and locked away. Hidden where they couldn't be seen or hurt. What would it take to break through that fortress?

"We should get all of this cleared up and washed." She stood, quieter than Cadence had, and started to pick up plates.

"I'll help." I stood and followed her to the kitchen.

Chapter Nine

Oaklyn

GRAN DISAPPEARED INTO THE TV ROOM AT THE back of the house, leaving Nate and I in the dimly lit kitchen.

"She doesn't like to waste electricity," I explained, gesturing up at the only can light in the centre of the ceiling. The bulb was one of those energy-saving ones.

"I like it like this." Nate placed the dishes beside the sink and started to fill it with hot water from the faucet, and a squirt of the dish soap from the bottle he pulled out of the cabinet.

"You don't have to do that," I said as he started to roll up his sleeves, revealing skin covered with tattoos.

He flashed me a grin that threatened to make me reconsider a whole bunch of life choices.

"I said I would," he said easily. "You can dry." Hands in the steaming, soapy water, he started to wash each dish carefully, one by one.

I watched for a moment before grabbing up a towel and starting to swipe it over the dishes as he handed them to me.

"You must think I'm a train wreck," I said.

"I don't think that." He carefully scrubbed inside of the bowl Cadence ate her chowder from. "Why would I think that?"

I grunted softly. "Let me count the ways. First of all, my grandmother is a fruit loop."

"I think she's epic," he said. He handed me the bowl and leaned his hip against the counter. Grimaced, then drew away to reveal a patch of water on the side of his jeans. "I might have splashed a bit too vigorously."

"Are you sure that's just water?" I teased.

He looked back up at me and grinned again. "With you around, who can say? I almost came a couple of times watching you eat that lobster roll."

My face hot, I turned to place the bowl on the stack in the open shelf beside the window. "Nate—"

He grabbed the corner of the towel and dried his

fingers before tugging it, and me, towards him. "I like hearing you say my name."

"We can't do this," I whispered. I pulled the corner of the fabric from his hand, dried a plate and turned to place it on the stack beside the bowls.

Nate stepped behind me, his hands to either side of me on the countertop. Pinning me in. He leaned in, over my shoulder. His breath made my neck tingle.

"Oaklyn." He spoke in a soft whisper, barely audible, my name brushing my ear as it slid off his lips like silk. "I know you want me as much as I want you."

Pressed against me as he was, I felt him harden against my hip. Breathing became difficult. Thinking was almost impossible. The only thing left was to feel. The length of his body against me. My heart racing, threatening to claw its way out of my chest. A rapid throbbing that started in my clit and radiated through every part of me.

He nuzzled his face into the side of my throat, inhaling the scent of me. Could he smell how turned on I was? How could he not? I was standing on the edge of a knife, waiting to plunge down the other side. Not knowing where I might land.

"I know things are complicated," he whispered.

"But not everything has to be. Not everything is. This is simple. You and I."

He pressed his mouth to my neck, teasing my sensitive skin with his tongue. Slowly, he licked from my collarbone, up my neck and across to my throat.

I shivered. Surrendering would be so easy. Gran had the TV up so loud she wouldn't hear us. And Cadence... We could be quiet so we didn't disturb her. I might have to cover my mouth to keep myself from screaming his name, but we could...

Then his mouth was gone and the rest of him as he stepped away from me.

I took a moment to gather my thoughts before turning around and leaning against the countertop, careful this section was dry. It was. The only thing wet was my panties.

"We should get the rest of these done." His hands were back in the sink, deftly washing the last couple of plates and spoons.

"You were right about one thing," I said.

"What's that?" He handed me another plate to dry.

"You are good at washing up," I said.

"You seem surprised." He raised a teasing eyebrow at me. "Did you think I was exaggerating my dishwashing prowess?"

"When you put it that way..." I wiped the plate dry and put it away, careful not to turn my back on him again. "You strike me as the kind of guy who'd have a dishwasher."

"I do," he said. He washed the cutlery and pulled the plug out of the sink. "I didn't always."

Careful to choose a dry spot himself, he leaned against the counter again and regarded me. "I grew up in Highball Creek. My mother was a teacher. My dad drove a truck. When he was sober enough, which wasn't all that often." He glanced down at the linoleum on the kitchen floor. "We never had much money. We lived in a tiny two-bedroom house. I shared a room with my brother and sister, and we couldn't afford a dishwasher."

He looked back up and gave me a cheeky smile. "I learned to clean dishes before I could walk."

I snorted a laugh. "I'm sure you did. And now you live in Lowball Bay, playing professional hockey." And earning more money than he'd know what to do with.

"Now I have a house on Hardball Ridge, over-looking the bay, with more rooms than I could ever fill. It feels empty."

"You miss your family," I said.

"I miss how close we were," he said. "I don't miss

my brother snoring. Or my sister talking in her sleep," he said.

"Where are they now?" I asked.

"My brother, Rhys, is a self-made billionaire, believe it or not," Nate said. "He started off as a nerd, trying to find a way to make plastic break down faster. Now, he owns a huge company that provides environmental solutions to countries all over the world."

My eyes widened. "That's pretty amazing." Of course, I should have put two and two together. Anyone who lived in the city knew who Rhys Southwell was. Especially given he'd been widowed relatively young and left with two children. Nate's nieces.

"I guess it's a bit more impressive than hitting a puck around the ice with a stick." Nate said with a shrug.

"Entertaining people is amazing too, and playing professional ice hockey takes a lot of skill," I reminded him. As if he needed a reminder. No doubt he was well aware of the fact.

"What about your sister?" I asked before he could preen too much. "Let me guess, she invented the cure for every disease imaginable and she's now a trillionaire?"

"She still lives in Highball Creek," he said. "She's married to a carpenter and they have a bunch of kids. She might be the happiest one of all of us."

"Right." The ache in my heart was almost painful. When I was Cadence's age, all I wanted was to get married and have a bunch of kids. I wanted to find a man who loved me the way my father loved my mother. The way I *thought* he loved her. Before I knew about Cadence and my world fell down around my ears.

"You want kids someday," I said. Of course he did. Living in a house that big, it would take at least four or five to fill it.

"I don't know," he said slowly. "I guess so. Maybe."

"You don't know?" I asked. "Of course you don't, you're still a kid yourself." I couldn't resist the tease.

He picked up the towel from where I placed it on the counter and threw it at me. I caught it and flung it back at him.

He grabbed it out of the air and held one end, flicking at me with the other.

I laughed and danced out of the way. "See what I mean? Just a kid."

"There's a difference between being a kid and acting like one," he said. "Just so you know, I can be a mature adult if I want to." He folded the towel and placed it back down neatly.

"I think I'd like to be a kid again," I said reflectively. "It would be nice to be seven or eight. When all you have to worry about is what game to play next. Or who to invite to your birthday party."

"Or having to explain to your mother that you crashed another bike and skinned your knees. Again," he said.

I shook my head at him.

He grinned. "What? Don't tell me you never crashed a bike. Or skinned your knees." His smile turned teasing. "Or got carpet burn?" His gaze dropped to my knees.

"I never crashed a bike," I said.

When I didn't say any more, he looked up, an eyebrow raised. "You're not denying the other two."

"No, I'm not," I agreed. "What kid hasn't grazed their knees?"

"And the carpet burn?" He took a step closer, eyes eager for an explanation. "There has to be a story there. Let me guess, college dorm?"

"I didn't go to college," I said. That was never in the cards for me. I couldn't have stayed still for three or four years. After the first, I would have wanted to move on to something else, or somewhere else.

"Then—?" he prompted.

"Oaklyn, can you make me a cup of tea?" Gran roared from the back of the house.

"Sure, Gran," I called back. I winced, remembering Cadence was in the house, possibly trying to sleep. Or at least, lying awake trying to get her head together. Either way, I might have to insist Gran text me, rather than us yelling. Assuming my sister was here for long enough for us to change our routine.

I shrugged. "Saved by the bell. Or belle, with an E."

"I still want that story out of you," he said. He shook his finger at me as though telling me he wouldn't forget.

I turned on Gran's electric kettle, her only concession when it came to modern appliances. While the water started to boil, I grabbed a cup and teabag.

"I should thank you," I said. "For bringing us dinner and being here for me during this...craziness. You've been a good friend." Although, none of my friends had ever pressed themselves against me and tasted my neck before. Never drove me to the edge of surrender, until I was almost begging for their touch.

He reached up to brush hair off the side of my

face and tuck it behind my ear. "We're more than friends, Oaklyn."

"Nate," I whispered. "I know you want more." His touch sent electricity all the way through me, right to my core.

At the same time I was acutely aware of Cadence and Gran and all the complications that came with both of them, and my life in general. I couldn't be the woman he wanted me to be, even if I tried. I was a clusterfuck in ways he had no idea about. Ways I could barely bring myself to think about.

"I know you want more too," he said. He leaned in, until his mouth was beside my ear. "You're mine." That was all he said before he pulled away and stepped back. "I'll see you at work in the morning."

Before I could put together a coherent response, he was gone.

Chapter Ten

Nate

Blake leaned forward as far as his seatbelt would allow and turned to look at me.

I looked back at him. Raised my eyebrows.

"What?" I should have known better than to ask, but I never could resist. What was the point when he'd keep being weird until I asked anyway?

"Do I have something on my face?" I knew I didn't. I checked in the washroom mirror before boarding the plane. Coach Lampton and the team's general manager, Hamish Ross, wouldn't appreciate it if any of us looked messy in public. Not when we were supposed to be representing the Sea Dragons.

"I've seen that look before," Blake said.

"Yeah, it's called a smile," I said. "It's been

known to happen to one of us every now and again. Some more than others."

Blake squinted. "Nah, there's more to it than that. I've seen that expression most recently on..." He looked up and down the aisle beside him before turning back to me. He mimed a drum roll. "Mr. Cameron North."

"What does Cam have to do with this?" I asked. I knew where this was going, but I couldn't help trying to deflect it in a different direction anyway.

"I think the most important question here is, who is responsible for the smile on your face?" Blake said. He held a pretend microphone in front of my mouth like he was interviewing me. "Nathaniel Southwell, who are you in love with?"

"Apart from you?" I teased, leaning forward to speak into the pretend microphone.

He drew the 'mic' back in front of his bearded face. "You heard it here first, folks." His head bobbed back and forth like the bobble head version of him they sold in the Sea Dragons' arena gift store.

They sold one of me too. It was a thing of nightmares. For one thing, I was better looking, and not made out of plastic. If course, I owned a couple of them. They were scattered around my house. During parties, they were an interesting talking point.

I gave one to my nieces and nephews as well. According to my sister, one of my nephews loved it so much he wouldn't stop shaking and watching the head bounce back and forth. Until one day, the head fell off and rolled across the floor. She said my nephew screamed his lungs out.

Like I said, a thing of nightmares. Fortunately, my nephew hadn't tried that with the real me. Yet.

"Everyone knows you're head over heels for me. Like everyone else in the team." Blake wiggled his eyebrows and pulled out his phone to take a quick selfie. He leaned over so we could take one together before he dropped his phone in the seat pocket in front of him.

"I'm not," Zack said from the seat in front of us. "I think you're an idiot."

"He's in denial," Blake said loudly.

"Of course he is." There was no arguing with Blake or Zack, but I might as well enjoy the moment where the conversation wasn't about me. I'd rather talk about them all the way to the West Coast, rather than discuss my life. Especially my love life. "I'm sure he'll catch up eventually."

"In your fucking dreams," Zack said.

Blake spread his hands out to either side and shrugged. "I guess there's no accounting for bad taste. Speaking of taste, we were talking about you. Is it Ursula from reception? You'd be cute together."

I couldn't say the pink-haired woman wasn't cute, but I'd seen her in the arena café, holding hands with Jenny from the accounting department. "I don't think her girlfriend would agree." I wasn't sure if that's how they were to each other, officially, but it would get the message across to Blake that nothing was going on between me and her. And never would.

Blake looked disappointed, but rallied so quickly I knew he was toying with me. "Okay, then it has to be the blonde from the staff gym. Oaklyn Walsh."

"Maybe it is and maybe it isn't," I said, trying to play it cool and cagey.

"I was there when you first met her, remember?" he said. "I know smitten at first sight when I see it. You, sir, are smitten." He pointed an accusing finger at my chest before poking me with it.

I swatted his hand away. "And what if I am? Are you jealous or something?" He had no trouble getting the attention of women wherever he went. Sooner or later, he'd find one who'd put up with his quirks. And his pranks.

For the record, it's a good idea not to leave a bag unattended in his proximity. If you do, you might come back to your skates laced backwards, or beef jerky in your underwear. Once, he smeared Vaseline all over the visor of one of the left wingers and sprinkled glitter all over it. It looked amazing, but took some doing to wash it all off.

He poked me in the chest a couple more times before dropping his hand into his lap. "Bro, I'm happy for you. I never thought I'd see the day when Nate Southwell would be in love for more than a day or two. Or three."

"People can change," I said, more tersely than I intended. Sure, my reputation as a player was deserved, but that wasn't all I was about. I wasn't just a stick with a dick. I had a heart that beat for a blond woman in body fitting lycra.

I got the impression she thought she wasn't worthy of being loved, but she was wrong. She was more than worthy. She deserved to be worshiped like the goddess she was. And I was just the guy to do the worshiping.

"Some people can," Blake agreed. "Some people don't want to. You seemed happy the way you were. You know what they say, if it ain't broke, don't fix it."

"I was happy," I said. "I am... I wasn't broken, I just like her, okay?"

"Some people would say we're all broken, one way or another," he said with his head tilted as though he was some wise philosopher. I presumed he learned that from his therapist. "Does she like you too?"

"What? Of course she does," I said.

He looked like he didn't believe me. Maybe I'd spoken a bit too quickly, like I was trying to convince myself.

"Bro—" he started.

It was my turn to poke him in the chest with my finger. "Don't start with me, Eastwood. I like her and she likes me. We're going to be together. That's all you need to know." I gave him an extra poke for good measure.

He patted the side of my hand sympathetically. "We're here for you when you need help picking up the pieces. I'm sure the Casey twins would be happy to help you out too."

I batted his hand away. "I don't need the fucking Casey twins, okay?"

"Someone else then," he said. "What about that girl who gave you a blowjob in the..." He must have seen my face turn red, because he actually stopped speaking, which was a first for him.

"I don't want anyone else," I said, fighting the urge to lose my shit. On the ice, I'd take a swing, but I couldn't do that in a plane, and not with a teammate.

Someone would take photos and they'd end up plastered all over the Internet by the time we landed. That would be followed by a reprimand, a fine and maybe a suspension.

It wouldn't be worth it. Not when Blake more or less meant well. "And I don't need you to worry about me or my love life."

Cam stopped at our row on the way past, his hand beside Blake's head. "Since when do you have a love life?" he asked.

I thumped my head against the seat behind me. "Don't you fucking start."

"Nate is in love." Blake drew the word out until he ran out of breath.

"Huh. For how long?" Cam teased. "A week or two?"

Blake laughed and offered Cam a fist bump.

"You guys fucking suck," I told them. "I'm not that guy anymore." I wasn't ashamed of my past, but that wasn't me now. Not since the moment I first saw Oaklyn. One glance and I was changed forever.

Blake looked skeptical, but Cam at least had the decency to lean over and offer me a fist bump.

"I'm happy for you, bro. Being in love is one of the best things that ever happened to me." He smiled, that goofy expression he got when he was thinking about Andi.

I was happy for him, but it was a bit weird, given she was basically the boss. Sometimes it felt a bit like watching my parents get together. Honestly, though, they were good for each other. He was less grumpy than he used to be. I'd bet just about anything they'd get married and live happily ever after.

Blake made a gagging sound.

"Blake is jealous because no one would want to fall in love with him," I said. If he was going to keep taking digs at me, then I was going to give as good as I got.

"Someone might some day," Cam said. "As long as it's not my sister, Alice, then I'll be happy for him too." He gave Blake a meaningful look, eyes narrowed, like he might tear him a new one if he went anywhere near her.

Cam gave me a nod before heading back to his seat.

Blake looked after him thoughtfully.

"I'm pretty sure he meant that," I said warningly. "He's pretty protective of her."

"She's cute," Blake said with a shrug.

"Bro." I tipped my head back and looked up at the ceiling. "You like walking on the edge."

"I prefer skating on the edge," he said. "Don't worry about me; she hates my guts. She doesn't understand my need to enjoy life. She told me I was the biggest pain in her ass, like ever."

"I wonder why?" I said sarcastically.

"Me too," he said with a mock pout. "You have a sister, don't you?"

"A *married* sister," I reminded him. "And if she wasn't, I would let you near her either." She had four kids, she didn't need him to be her fifth.

"Fair enough," he said. "I wouldn't let you near mine."

"You don't have a sister," I pointed out.

"No, but if I did, I'm sure she wouldn't be your type." He adjusted his seatbelt and leaned back. Lacing his hands behind his head, he closed his eyes.

"You mean you wouldn't want her near a fuck boy?" I asked.

"That too," he said without opening his eyes. "No offense."

"Offense taken," I said under my breath. "How long are you going to keep thinking that about me?"

He turned his head slightly and cracked his eyelids apart. "You never had a problem with it before."

"I have a problem with it now," I said.

I grabbed my headphones out of the seat pocket and rammed them down over my ears. Tapping the screen of my watch, I turned on my playlist.

If I had the music up loud enough, it might drown out the sound of my reputation. And let me focus on thinking about Oaklyn and the way she tasted. The way her body felt pressed against me. The way her breath caught when I told her she was mine. Even the caring way she took care of her grandmother and the sister she barely knew. Everything about her left me wanting to know more. The next couple of weeks traveling across the continent were going to feel like forever.

In the corner of my eye, I saw Blake trying to say something, but I ignored him. I didn't care if he was trying to apologize or make things worse. I just wanted to sit back and try to enjoy the rest of the flight to Los Angeles.

Chapter Eleven

Oaklyn

"Do we have to do this?" Cadence looked down at the Lowball Bay version of Monopoly, her lip curled in dismay.

I leaned over and whispered, "Just roll with it." I pulled out a chair and lowered myself into it.

"Dibs on the humpback." Gran pulled the lid off the box and reached in for the token. "Oaklyn, you can have the sea dragon." She slid it across the table to me.

I caught it and rolled my eyes at her. Of course she'd suggest that. She never could help herself.

"Which one do you want?" I asked Cadence.

She looked at me like she didn't want any of them, but reluctantly plopped down into a chair and leaned her crossed arms on the table top. "Is there a phone?"

Gran laughed. "No, there's not a phone. There's a starfish, a grouper and a sea cucumber."

"If I have to play, I'll have the starfish," Cadence said. "The others sound as lame as the game."

Gran clicked her tongue. "I'll have you know they're all mascots for the sporting teams here in the city. This one is the NBA team." She tossed the starfish to Cadence.

Cadence caught it and looked down at it. "That's super weird."

"You said 'super awesome' wrong," Gran said.

"No, I didn't," Cadence contradicted. "Are we playing or not?"

"That's the spirit." Gran grinned as though Cadence wasn't being sarcastic. She unfolded the board and counted out our pretended money before cupping the dice in her hand and throwing them onto the table. "Six! Hell yeah." She counted the spaces and moved her token.

"Why are we doing this?" Cadence asked as Gran handed her the dice.

"Family bonding," Gran said. "Nothing says togetherness like me whipping both of your asses. Now go ahead and roll them there dice."

"Can't we play a real game?" Cadence asked. She shook the dice in her hand and dropped them half-heartedly on the table.

"Are you referring to computer games?" Gran asked. "I haven't played one of those since *Space Invaders*. Have they developed much since then?" The mischief in her eyes said she was joking, but Cadence rolled her eyes.

"*Space Invaders* is a classic now," I said. "So is *Pong*."

Gran waited until Cadence moved her starfish two spaces before saying, "This gets us talking to each other, but if you want, I can whip your ass in *Super Mario Kart* after this."

Cadence immediately perked up. "Can we play that instead?"

"Let's see if we can beat Gran at this first," I said. "She doesn't win all the time."

"Do too," Gran said.

"Do not," I said. I shook the dice and threw a ten. "See? I'm winning already." I gave them both a smug smile before moving my token ahead of theirs.

"Lucky throw," Gran said. Of course, she had to get an eleven next.

Were the Sea Dragons themselves as competitive as she was? Come to think of, was *anyone* as competitive as my grandmother? She loved nothing more than winning and bragging about it afterward.

Cadence was quick to scoop up the dice and take her turn. "Twelve, yes! We just have to get to the other end of the board first, right?" She leaned forward to move her token quickly.

Gran stared at her. "Are you trying to tell me you don't know how this game works?"

I groaned softly. I was hoping she'd humor Cadence and let us stop playing when one of us got our token all the way around the board. Of course, I should have known better. When Gran decided it was family bonding time, no one got off without the full experience.

"I knew your father was an asshole, but I had no idea how deep it went," Gran declared.

"Gran!" I looked at her in horror. Not just because it was only a board game, but because Cadence was right there, still fragile. Still grieving. And me? All the darkest memories came flooding back in the last couple of days. All of the wounds were raw again, like they'd just been inflicted.

"She's not wrong," Cadence softly. "My mother used to tell me how much I was like him."

Her words were met with a hollow silence. Even Gran understood she'd said too much this time. At least, she seemed to. She was speechless for once. For now.

I leaned over to lightly touch Cadence's elbow with my fingertips. "You are not like him." I was tempted to try to hug her, but we weren't at that point yet. So far, she hadn't shown any inclination towards physical affection of any kind. Maybe she just didn't like it. I guessed we had that in common. I wondered how many other ways we were alike.

"Aren't I?" She looked down at my hand. "I look like him. So do you. He ran away from your mother. I ran away from my foster parents."

"Those two aren't the same things," I said. But she scored a bullseye with her observation. If there was anything I was good at, it was running away. I never thought about comparing myself to him though. Not until she said the words. I pushed the thoughts aside for now. She needed me more than I needed to wallow.

"He left my mom because their marriage was over," I said. Because he ended it by cheating on her and having another family. "You came here because you wanted to be with family. That makes you the exact opposite of him."

"He left your family so he could be with mine," she pointed out. "That makes us the same. Like Gran said, I'm the asshole here." Her eyes glittered with unshed tears.

"I never said you were the asshole," Gran said, uncharacteristically gruff. "I said he was the asshole. There's no need for you to decide I was insinuating anything about you."

I was starting to feel family bonding night rapidly unraveling. "Maybe we could all take a breath and calm down." I wished Nate was here. He would have known what to say to defuse the conversation. A well-timed joke, or some word of wisdom. Something other than inhale and exhale a couple of times and chill out. He was much better at this family thing than I was. Of course he was, he had siblings he grew up with and nieces and nephews around. All I had was a grandmother with no filter and a mother who checked out on me when my father checked out on her.

"Maybe we could stop playing this stupid game," Cadence said.

I wasn't sure if she was referring to the board game or the situation. The fact it might be both broke my heart.

"Cadence," I said softly, "if you don't want to play anymore, you don't have to. We just thought it might be fun." We should have started with *Super*

Mario Kart. Or maybe a nice walk around the neighborhood. It was cold out, but if we walked fast enough, we would have warmed up soon enough.

Cadence shoved her chair back hard enough to rock the table and dislodge the tokens. "I'll be in my room."

She stomped away, leaving us to sit in silence.

"That girl is—" Gran raised her finger.

"Don't start," I growled. "She's been through hell. The last thing she needs is for us to bring up Dad, much less say horrible things about him."

"True things," Gran said darkly. "You're not going to defend him, are you?"

"What are you going to do if I am?" I asked. "Kick me out?" I closed my eyes and took the deep breaths I'd recommended a couple of minutes earlier.

"I have no intention of defending him," I said finally. I opened my eyes and stared her down. "This has nothing to do with him. I know you hate him. I get it. He broke Mom's heart. I remember you flying over to see her. I remember her crying. But that was a lifetime ago. What matters now is that kid in there and how she's hurting." I jerked my head towards the closed door to Cadence's room.

Gran leaned forward. "Have you ever heard the

saying 'the apple doesn't fall far from the tree'? It's typical of him to up and die, and dump her on you."

"That wasn't what happened," I said.

I was still waiting for social services to contact me about her. The longer it took, the more attached to her I got. But I kept telling myself I had no business trying to parent a teenager. Tonight was another example of how bad I was at it. I couldn't defuse a situation that somehow I should have seen coming a mile away. I should have suggested we do something else tonight. Board games were known to cause aggravation amongst players, especially Gran. And Cadence hadn't wanted to play to start with. I should have listened.

I could have unraveled a long list of things I should and shouldn't have done and let it roll all the way across the floor and out the door. What it came down to was I had no clue what I was doing. Not one. I couldn't even guess what Nate would have done. Whatever it was, it would have been better than this.

"Close enough," Gran said with petulance that would have matched Cadence's.

"She's not her father," I said. "In case you've forgotten, he's my father too."

Gran grunted. "You're your mother's daughter."

"That's convenient," I said sarcastically. "If I had a different mother, you'd hate me too then?"

She looked downright offended. "I don't hate you. I don't hate the kid either."

"Then what's the problem?" I shook my head at her. "Because you certainly seem to have one." She never held back on speaking her mind before, why would she start now?

"How do you think your mother would feel if she knew Cadence was here?" Gran asked.

My mouth dropped open like I was a fish just pulled out the bay. That was definitely not what I expected to hear.

"Mmm, didn't think of that did you?" she asked. "I can tell by your face that her coming here dredged up a lot of shit. It'd do the same to your mother. I don't want her to hurt any more than she's already been."

She was as protective of her daughter as she was competitive. I couldn't remember her ever being this protective of me. Was that because I'd decided to be fiercely independent from the moment I found out what he did? I'd been the one to comfort my mother when he left and Gran returned to Lowball Bay. I was the one who cooked dinner and made sure she ate. I was the one who got myself up in the mornings and off to school. Maybe it looked like I didn't care, but I did.

Deep down in my soul, I did.

"No one wants her hurt," I said quietly. "But she's a grown woman. I can't tell a sixteen-year-old that she has to go back where she came from because it might hurt my mother's feelings. I'm sure as hell not going to tell her she has to leave because of my feelings. If that's what you think, then maybe she and I should be the ones to leave."

I pushed my chair back hard and stalked to the kitchen to make myself a cup of tea. The sound of the feet screeching on the floor rang in my ears for a couple of moments afterwards. I turned on the kettle and grabbed out a box of chamomile tea, but not before I noticed Cadence's door closing all the way.

She must have stood there listening to every word we said.

Chapter Twelve

Nate

Oaklyn was already in the gym when I arrived in the morning. She was off to the side, setting up for the lunchtime yoga class that took place on a Tuesday. No, I totally hadn't memorised her routine. *Cough.*

Anyway, she looked tired and frustrated, shaking out the yoga mats with more vigor than I would have thought was necessary.

"Do you need a hand?" I offered. I pulled off my hoodie and put it aside on the weight bench with my phone.

She glanced over at me. "I'm good." She proceeded to pull out a third mat and shake the crap out of it before laying it on the floor and adjusting it so it was perfectly parallel to the other two.

"So I see." I leaned against the wall beside her and crossed my ankles. "How are things going with Cadence?"

"About the same." She grabbed a fourth mat and started trying to unravel it. It stubbornly stayed rolled up. She growled in annoyance and tried again, harder this time.

"Let me," I said. I stepped away from the wall, took the mat from her hands and unrolled it carefully before setting it down with the rest.

"Thanks," she said, her teeth gritted. "I can't get anything right today."

"I'm sure that's not true." I unrolled the last two mats and placed them beside the others.

I wanted to drag her down to a mat and taste her between her legs. I bet her pussy was delicious and the sound she made when she came was better than I could imagine. If it wasn't for the impending yoga class, I might have tried. Maybe I'd stick around until after the class was over. Giving her an orgasm with my mouth would be worth being late for practice.

"I tried to make toast for breakfast for me and Cadence and burnt it," she said. "I forgot to put coffee in the coffee machine, so all I got was hot water. I had to push my car to get it to start, so I could get Cadence to school. Gran was in the driver's seat, steering," she added quickly.

"I had to drive around the block three times to find somewhere to stop long enough to let Cadence out," she continued. "By the time I got here, I had to park two blocks away. Then I realized I left my keys in the car and had to go back for them. I'm pretty sure I'm illegally parked and I'm going to get towed away."

She took a frustrated breath. "And I just realized I left my lunch on the kitchen counter. I hope Cadence took hers with her." She massaged her forehead with her fingertips.

I stepped around behind her and started to rub her shoulders. "Hey, everyone has bad days. I've had my share of them."

"You won all of your away games," she said. She dropped her head forward and let me work out her knots for her.

"You're keeping track," I said, allowing myself a smug smile.

"I work in an ice hockey stadium," she said dryly. "I couldn't avoid it if I tried."

"Ouch," I said playfully. "Are you trying to say you're avoiding me?"

"I've tried, but it doesn't seem to work," she said. "You keep on coming back."

"Yes I do." She was so tense. I worked out the knot in one shoulder and started on the other. "I'm never going to stop coming back." All this talk about coming had my cock hardening.

"You should," she said. "I've told you, I'm a train wreck. You know those little crochet dumpster fires? That's me too. Excuse my language, but I'm a category five shitstorm."

She was adorable when she apologised for swearing. I'd noticed she rarely did it. It didn't bother me if she dropped an F bomb every sentence, but it was totally up to her. It was another aspect of her, and I hadn't found one I didn't like yet.

"You are none of those things," I said. "You're cuter than a pedal-powered car driven by pink monkeys."

She laughed and looked back at me over her shoulder. "That's strangely specific."

I grinned. "What can I say? I'm a strangely specific guy. Some would say, just strange."

Right now, I'd prefer that to some of the other things people assumed about me. With irritation, I thought back to my conversation with Blake on the flight to the West Coast. We hadn't talked about it since. I barely said a word to him while he acted like nothing happened. Typical Blake. He'd probably forgotten all about it by now. At least he hadn't made any further digs. Maybe I got through to him after all.

"You're not strange." She dropped her head back down. "I made a mess of things with Cadence the other night. And Gran." She explained about family bonding night, not going into much depth, except to explain she fought with her grandmother, and Cadence overheard.

"All families have their arguments," I said. "My sister and I used to stick string to the wall in the bedroom to mark off my section from hers. If anyone crossed that string, they'd get a kick or a punch."

"How many times did you cross the string?" Oaklyn asked.

"Every chance I got." I smiled at the memory. She'd sit reading a book and I'd poke a toe over the line. Then the rest of my foot. Her favorite thing was waiting until I was far enough over to stomp as hard on my foot as she could.

"Why am I not surprised?" Oaklyn said. "What about your brother? Was there a piece of string for his section too?"

My smile faded. "Yeah, but we didn't cross that

one. He would have told our father and my father had a temper. He never raised a hand to any of us, but he was good at yelling. Teasing Rhys wasn't worth it."

"It sounds like you had a nice childhood, for the most part," Oaklyn said. She sounded wistful.

"You didn't?" I asked. "Before your dad did what he did, I mean. You must have some good memories."

"I suppose I do," she said after a few moments of thought. "We used to go down to Pike Place, to the markets there. We'd wander through the tables and look at everything. Then he'd buy me an ice cream and we'd sit and look at the water while we ate them. After that, we'd walk over to the Space Needle and go up inside it. I could have stood and looked at the view for hours. Funny, every time there's water, I find my way there. No matter where I go."

"Me too." I stopped massaging her shoulders and instead ran my thumbs up and down the sides of her neck. "Where else have you been?"

"All over," she said. "I've even spent some time in Stickville, Illinois." She was teasing me now, because she must have known the Danglers were one of the Sea Dragons biggest rivals.

"Traitor," I said jokingly. "If the next words out

of your mouth on it you have a jersey from one of the players on the roster there..."

"You'll do what?" she asked.

"I'll take it," I said. "I'll give it to Blake to run up the flagpole the next time they come here to play. To send a message." I leaned in to whisper. "My woman only wears my jersey. Number six."

She shivered. "Is that right?"

I ran my hands down her arms and around to her stomach, wrapping my arms around her. "That's right." She smelled like shampoo and lavender soap.

"What if I don't want to wear your jersey?" she asked.

I laughed, letting her feel my body rumbling against hers. "Then you can go naked."

Now I was hard as a rock, picturing her completely bare. Her perky breasts ready for me, nipples hard, aching to be sucked. Did the curls at the apex of her thighs match her golden blond hair?

"Nate..." She shook her head. "What am I going to do about my sister? I got a text this morning that social services will call me tomorrow. I don't even know what to say to them."

"What do you want to say?" I asked.

"I don't know," she admitted. "Part of me wants to insist she stay with me, but I'm not sure that's what she needs. That's the most important thing here. What's best for her. It's not about me or my ego. What I want doesn't matter."

I unwound myself from her, turned her around and cupped her cheeks with my hands. I looked right into her blue eyes, so stormy right now. So troubled.

"You're wrong," I told her. "What you want matters a lot. You're not a train wreck or a dumpster fire. You're a beautiful woman who's doing the best you can with a complicated situation. One that most people don't have to face in their lifetime. As far as I know, teenagers don't turn up on your doorstep on the regular. I mean, it's never happened to me."

If I'd fathered any children, I was unaware of it. Given my public status, it was likely the mother would have come forward, wanting support, even if it was just financial. Which, for the record, I would have totally been on board with.

Although, I would have wanted to be in my kid's life too. I couldn't imagine having a mini-me out there and not being there for them. If I had a kid, I wanted to teach them how to skate and play hockey. And if they wanted to do something else, I'd be behind them all the way.

"The point is, you need to stop beating yourself up about every little thing. So, sometimes things go wrong, so what? That happens to everyone. None of us are perfect."

"Not even you?" She raised an eyebrow slightly, like she was expecting me to say that of course I was. Not even Zack or Blake were that arrogant. Mostly.

I snorted. "Especially not me." Which, once again, brought me back to the conversation with Blake. "I've made mistakes that follow me wherever I go." Not that I regretted any of my past encounters, just that I gave the guys too many opportunities to give me shit.

"Yeah?" She looked hopeful. "Like what?"

"Like not throwing you over my shoulder and carrying you away." I lowered my shoulder as though I might do that.

She stepped back and raised her hands in front of her. "Don't you dare. The lunch class will be here any minute now." Even as she said the words, she laughed. The weight on her when I'd walked into the gym had lessened a little now. Not gone completely, but not as heavy.

I straightened up and grinned. "If you think that would stop me, you better think again, woman. I won't, but only because you asked me nicely." I looked at her sideways. "You did ask me nicely, right?"

She gave me a 'really,' look, but then said, "Don't pick me up," she said. "Please."

My voice low and husky, I said, "I like it when you say please." And then I got to enjoy the way her face turned pink. She was so fucking adorable I wanted to carry her out of here anyway. I couldn't wait to hear her begging for my cock. Begging for me to fuck her.

"What time did social services say they'd call?" I said, hating having to bring all of this back down to earth.

Her face went from pink to slightly white. "Two thirty p.m."

"I'll be here," I said.

"But you have training—" she started.

"I'll be here," I said again. "I promised to go through this with you and I will. We've got this, okay?"

I hoped like hell I did. If not, I'd be here to pick up the pieces.

Chapter Thirteen

Oaklyn

I waited for the phone to ring, my heart in my throat.

And waited.

"What's taking so long?" I stalked from one side of the gym to the other, while Nate, shirtless and sweaty, lifted weights.

"You said they were busy, didn't you?" He wasn't even out of breath. He lifted a hundred pounds like it was nothing. His skin was slick under the fluorescent lights. Tattoos gleaming.

"Yeah," I said. Reluctantly, because an appointment was an appointment. I hated to be late and hated when other people were late. Especially when it was something as important as this. Cadence's whole future was a big deal. Didn't they realize that?

I sucked in a breath. Of course they did. She wasn't the only kid who needed taking care of. She was one of the lucky ones. She had somewhere to stay while all of these things were decided.

"Ms. Walsh?" A woman about my age, with long dark hair, dark eyes and a septum ring stepped into the gym. "I'm Kymmie Jones. From social services. I was supposed to give you a call, but I thought I'd drop in on my way past instead." She glanced at Nate with a raised eyebrow before turning her attention back to me.

"Great, great," I stammered. "That's me. Please call me Oaklyn."

"I'm Nate," the defenseman offered.

"If you'll excuse us," Kymmie started.

"If it's okay, I'd prefer he stay," I said. "He's been supporting me and Cadence since she arrived in town."

"Oaklyn and I are engaged," Nate said cheerfully. "That makes me practically family."

My eyes snapped to him. What the heck was he doing? We weren't... I forced myself to rally quickly. Of course, Kymmie wouldn't discuss personal matters in front of someone who wasn't family. Still, I hoped I didn't look like deer caught in the headlights. After this, he was going to have some explaining to do.

"Your file doesn't mention a fiancé," Kymmie said, pulling a tablet from the large bag in her hand and frowning at the screen.

"It's new," Nate said. "I proposed last night. Of course, Oaklyn said yes immediately. She's been the one nagging me to make a commitment." He was having way too much fun with this.

I gave him a dry look, but managed a smile. "That's right. Nate has always had commitment issues. For a while now, I thought I'd never pin him down. But then he proposed and promised the biggest diamond I'd ever seen." Two could have fun, if he insisted.

"I can't wait to put it on your finger, cupcake." Nate grinned.

Cupcake?

"I can't wait either, honeybun," I said, batting my eyelashes at him. "I'm going to have to do extra weights just so I can raise my hand, the ring is going to be so big."

Kymmie cleared her throat. "Um, congratulations. We should get to discussing Cadence."

"Cadence is so excited she's getting a brother-in-law," Nate said. "You should have seen her face when I proposed."

I gave him another glance. He was laying it on a bit thick now. Cadence probably would have rolled her eyes and found something more interesting on her phone.

"So you live together?" Kymmie asked. "My understanding was that Oaklyn and Cadence were staying with Oaklyn's grandmother, uh, Ms. Henstridge." She checked her notes again.

"That's right," I said. "Those commitment issues again. He promised to have a key cut."

"Cupcake, my house doesn't need keys," Nate said. "I said I'd have a card made for you. You know, you just have to swipe it in front of the box beside the door. That's what Oaklyn calls it. You'd think modern technology hadn't been invented."

I was tempted to use technology and text him a selfie of me flipping him off. Or I could just do it in person, but not in front of the social worker.

"Lucky I have you to help me out," I said sweetly. "And you have someone to remind you not to drink sour milk that's been sitting in the fridge for three weeks."

"I've never kept milk in the fridge after its expiry date," he protested.

"Of course not, honeybun, because your mother always throws it out first. But now you have me to do that. And Cadence too. She's a very responsible sixteen-year-old."

"Oh, she'll be living with both of you?" Kymmie asked. She pulled out a stylus from the top of the tablet cover and made a note on the screen.

I glanced at Nate. This whole thing could easily get out of hand. Pretending we were engaged so he could hear the personal details was very different from moving in with him. Especially with Cadence in tow.

"Absolutely," Nate agreed. "She'll have her own bedroom and bathroom. And living area, but of course we hope she'll spend lots of time with us. We think family bonding is important."

I shot him a warning look, but he just grinned back at me. He was as shameless as Gran. Shoot, Gran. What was she going to say about all of this? No doubt, she'd find it hilarious.

"We do, that's why Nate invited my grandmother to live with us too," I said. If he could take this too far, then I might as well take it a step further.

"Gran will have her own in-law suite," Nate said. "Where we can keep a close eye on her, so she doesn't get too wild. Oaklyn's grandmother is quite a character."

That was an understatement.

As for Nate, it seemed like he had all of this figured out. I wasn't sure what to make of it. I didn't think he planned to say any of this, but the way Kymmie was frantically scribbling on her screen, we were getting more and more carved in stone. And I was trying not to surrender to panic.

"Mr.— Nate," Kymmie said awkwardly. "You're a professional hockey player, correct?"

"Guilty," he said with a nod.

Her tongue darted over her lips. "You travel a lot?"

"Yes, I do," he said carefully. "That's why I think it's a good idea for Gran to move in with us. To have an extra adult around when I'm not there."

I wasn't sure how legitimate that sentiment was. He was barely an adult, and Gran... She barely functioned as one.

Although, contradicting him now could mean they'd send Cadence back to Seattle. This arrangement might give her a somewhat dysfunctional family, but it would see her settled if I decided to leave town at the end of my time here. As a bonus, I'd feel better if Gran was renting from Nate than living in her house alone. Whether she'd agree to that or not was a different story.

"I see," Kymmie said. "There's a small matter of...how can I put this delicately?"

"According to social media I'm a slut who moves from woman to woman on a nightly basis," Nate said flatly. He squared his jaw, a flash of irritation crossing his face. "You shouldn't believe everything you read. I'm committed to Oaklyn. And Cadence. Anything else you need to know?"

Kymmie's face was slightly pink. "Um, no, I think that's everything. I'm going to need to see your home and speak to Cadence. If everything checks out, I see no reason why she can't stay with both of you. Of course, I have to take anything she says and the suitability of her living accommodation into consideration."

"Absolutely," Nate said cheerfully. "My door is always open. I was just going to help Oaklyn move in tonight. And Cadence too, of course."

"Right, of course," Kymmie echoed.

"Can I ask you something?" I asked tentatively. "Cadence's foster parents, back in Seattle. Did they... want her back?"

Kymmie busied herself, looking at her screen for a few moments. "Officially, I can't tell you much.

Except to say they requested she be removed." She pressed her lips together regretfully, but it didn't seem as though this was anything new to her. Shuffling kids from home to home was part of the gig. Not even the worst part either.

Kids went into the foster system for reasons that were much more confronting than Cadence's situation. To think kids went through more trauma than what she'd already experienced was heartbreaking.

I couldn't help the flash of anger that passed through me though. After everything Cadence went through, her foster parents were going to send her away? I wasn't sure if I was the right fit for her, but *asking* social services to take her away...

"She ended up in the right place, right cupcake?" Nate asked.

"Yeah," I said absently. "Yes, she did." What would have happened to her if she hadn't run away and come here? Would they have called me, asking me to take her? Or would they have placed her somewhere else? Maybe somewhere better than with me. She could have had foster siblings, and gone on not knowing I existed.

I hurt myself with that thought.

"Great, then I'll be in touch." Kymmie turned off her tablet and dropped it into her bag. "I'll give you a couple of days to get organized, then I'll carry out my inspection and interview with Cadence. Thank you for your time." She nodded to us both before hurrying out of the gym.

I sagged against the wall the moment she was out of sight. Relief warring with overwhelm. I took a couple of deep breaths to calm my racing mind, then rounded on Nate.

"What the hell was that? Why would you tell her we're engaged?"

He stood and grabbed a towel to wipe sweat from his chest and chiseled abs.

"Because Cadence needs a stable home life," he said.

"You think I can't give that to her?" I asked, fuming.

The moment the words left my lips, my flash of anger was gone.

He was right, I couldn't. I had no plans to stay in Lowball Bay once Lacey was back from maternity leave. I'd only half unpacked my suitcase as it was. I was thinking of trying Boston next, or maybe somewhere in Maine. The idea of putting down roots was terrifying, even if it was only until Cadence wasn't a minor anymore.

"Of course you can, cupcake." He stepped closer

to me. "I'm not backwards enough to think a kid can't have a perfectly happy life with a single mother. Or a sister and a step-grandmother. Families come in all shapes and sizes. This isn't about that. This is about me being there for you. And for her. So both of you can have time to figure things out. When you do, if you want to move out again…"

"You'll help me move?" I asked, knowing the answer. Once I was there, he'd have a hard time letting me go. Sooner or later, he'd have to.

My life wasn't here in this city, with him.

The problem was, I had no idea where it was. I had to figure it out, or I might lose Cadence forever.

If I could bring myself to be completely honest, I didn't want to lose him either.

That was the most terrifying thing of all. I wasn't supposed to get attached to him, but tell that to the organ that thudded hard in my chest. The more time I spent with him the more I liked him. Really liked him. More than I ever liked any man before.

That was another in a long list of reasons why I shouldn't stick around town. And another in the ever-growing list of reasons why I should.

Before he could come up with an evasive response, my phone buzzed. I pulled it out of my pocket and glanced at the screen.

"Shoot."

"What is it?" He looked worried now, his head tilted as he regarded me.

"It's Cadence's school. I need to get down there."

"I'll drive." He grabbed his shirt and jammed it down over his head.

Chapter Fourteen

Nate

"I'm sorry," I said for the third time.

"I said it's okay," Oaklyn said, also for the third time. Her expression suggested things were very much not okay.

We'd hurried all the way out to my SUV, only for me to realize I left my phone in the gym. Again.

I couldn't even use my forgetfulness as an excuse to Oaklyn this time. I just hadn't grabbed the device from where it was, on the weight bench. Maybe Coach Ortiz was right and I should have it stapled to my forehead. Then I'd remember to bring the fucking thing.

We'd had to hurry back so she could unlock the gym for me to run in and get it. That scored us a bunch of funny glances from people we passed. Any other time, I might have stopped to explain, but not today. The look on Oaklyn's face was enough to make me hurry the fuck up, faster than if I was on the ice, mid breakaway.

"What do you think they want to talk about?" I asked.

"They didn't say," she said. "Just that I needed to get down there." She sounded frantic.

I wanted to grab her hand and tell her everything would be okay, but the roads were busy and I didn't dare take my hands off the steering wheel. I'd slowed us down enough without getting into a crash. Not to mention that if Oaklyn was hurt, I'd never forgive myself.

It was close to three o'clock, so the traffic near the high school was heavier than usual. Buses were pulling in to collect students and take them home. Cars and pedestrians were dodging around them.

A couple of students ran across the road without stopping to glance and see if it was safe. I had to jam my foot down on the brake to keep from running into them.

My heart pounding, we skidded to a stop in the middle of the road. The students laughed and ran off.

"Idiots," I muttered under my breath. They

could have been badly hurt, or worse. If I killed them, I wouldn't forgive myself for that either. Even if they were the ones who darted out in front of me.

I was about to tap the gas when a few more students stepped out, eyes on their phones. I had to wait until they'd crossed the road before I could keep going.

"Kids these days." I shook my head. I chanced a glance at Oaklyn, but she wasn't laughing. She looked tense, like a guitar string ready to snap.

I looked back to the road and kept on driving, moving slowly in case anyone else stepped out in front of us.

I found us a place to park as close as I could get us, and carefully backed in. I'd barely turned off the engine when Oaklyn was getting out and waiting for me on a patch of grass beside the road.

That was progress. A few days ago, she would have run straight for the entrance without looking back to see if I was following. Of course I would be; I'd follow her anywhere. Not like a stalker or anything like that. More like an adoring puppy, hoping to be tossed a treat or a scratch once in a while. Hoping to be allowed to sleep on her bed, snuggled up with her.

At least I didn't shed all over the place.

"Should we hold hands?" I asked. If we were going to pretend to be engaged, we should show some affection to each other. Right?

She parted her plush lips and I was sure she was about to say no, but then she held out her hand.

"We should make this convincing."

I didn't need to be told twice. I laced my fingers in hers and pulled her in closer.

"Whatever you say, cupcake." Her hand was warm in mine, slightly damp from anxiety, but that didn't deter me. She could have been dripping with sweat and I wouldn't have pulled away.

Especially if I was the cause of all that perspiration.

"Come on, honeybun." She started walking.

Dragging me behind her she couldn't see the silly grin on my face. Touching her, being here as her fiancé, even if it was fake, I couldn't have dreamed this up.

Worry for Cadence itched at me, but I wouldn't be anywhere else. If we were going to pull this off, and get Cadence settled with Oaklyn, then I'd have to play the role of responsible adult slash parent figure. How hard could it be? I had lots of experience as the cool uncle. Cadence seemed to like me. Gran too.

When the rest of the guys on the team found out about this, they were going to laugh their asses off. If it shut them up about my past, then it'd be more than worth it.

We headed across the grass and up to the front gate. It stood open to let the students out for the day and the parents in. Mostly, a steady stream of students was heading away, laughing and shouting to each other. Those who weren't already on their phones that was.

We pushed our way past them and into the building.

Lowball Bay High was basically the same as any high school in America. Linoleum floors, walls covered in pin boards obscured with paper held in place by thumb tacks.

Through one doorway, I made out a room filled with desks. The undersides of each one was probably covered in a variety of gum. I couldn't tell from here if the desktops had initials carved in them or drawn on them, but if it was anything like my high school, they did.

I remembered getting into trouble for writing my initials and Cassie Keys, and surrounding them with a love heart. She was in the year above me and had legs for days. I wanted to take her to prom, but she was fixated on some guy on the football team. Last I heard, she was married to a farmer and had a pile of kids.

"This brings back memories of my high school," Oaklyn muttered.

"Good ones?" I asked.

The look she gave me in response clearly said they weren't, before she led me to the front office.

Cadence sat just inside, slouched on a chair, phone in her hand, neutral expression on her face.

"Cadence, what's going on?" Oaklyn asked. "Are you okay?"

She waved a hand towards the door marked with 'Principal's Office'. "Ask her."

"I believe Oaklyn was asking you," I said. Look at me being all parent-y and stuff.

Cadence gave me the typical side eye, along with a frown that clearly said, 'I thought you were the cool one.'

I *was* the cool one. Right?

"I'll speak to Principal George," Oaklyn said. "Stay here."

I thought she was talking to me until I realized she was talking to Cadence. I took that as an invitation to follow her in.

"I got a message to come here and talk about my

sister," Oaklyn said to the woman who sat behind the desk.

Principal George looked up at her. "Please, take a seat." She waved at the pair of chairs on the opposite side of the desk.

"Did Cadence do something wrong?" Oaklyn asked. "She's gone through a rough time for the last while and she's still settling into things. I'm sure whatever it was, it was—"

The principal cut her off mid-sentence. "I'm sorry if I gave you the impression she'd caused trouble. It's the opposite, in fact. As you know, we spent the last few days testing her to make sure she's in the right classes. She failed to explain she was in the accelerated classes in her previous school."

"Oh." Oaklyn blinked a couple of times. "You're not going to tell me we should send her straight to college, are you?" She glanced at me.

I shrugged. If that was the case, I'd be sure she got a scholarship, if I had to make one for her.

The principal laughed. "Not quite yet. But her scores are right at the top for her age. With your permission, we'll be placing her in a year higher than her peers. I understand the transition could be difficult. Surrounded by students a year older than herself. It can cause problems with adjusting and potentially being ostracised."

"I already am," Cadence called out from the other room. "Everyone here thinks I'm weird."

"All the best people are weird," I called back. "Like me."

"Excuse me if you don't mind me asking," Principal George said slowly, giving me a speculative look.

"I'm Oaklyn's fiancé," I said.

From behind me came the sound of Cadence's phone hitting the floor. I imagined her jaw doing the same. We were going to have some explaining to do when this meeting was over.

"Ah, well, that's good," the principal said. She seemed genuinely approving.

It didn't take a genius to figure out why. "I don't want to throw my weight around," I said. "The other kids should like Cadence because she's awesome, not because she knows a professional hockey player or two."

"Who's the other one?" Cadence asked, hanging inside the doorway.

"You'll meet them at the engagement party," I said on-the-fly. "After I buy your sister the biggest rock she's ever seen." If either of them thought I wasn't completely serious about that, they were in for a surprise. If it helped to pull this off, I'd buy a ridiculously large diamond and put it on Oaklyn's finger myself.

"We don't need a big engagement party, honeybun," Oaklyn said.

"Of course we do, cupcake," I told her. "Everyone should be there to see how much you mean to me."

Cadence made a gagging sound.

Oaklyn forced a smile. "If you say so, honeybun. Anyway, now we have something else to celebrate. Cadence is doing so well she's been accelerated already."

"We can make it a double celebration," I said.

"Can we have cake?" Cadence asked.

"Any flavor you want," I promised.

"And clam chowder?" she asked.

"Absolutely," I said. "Any flavor of chowder you want." I was going to have to figure out when the hell I was going to have time to fit in a party. At this time of the season, we were busy nonstop. Practicing, traveling. Traveling and practicing. When we weren't doing those things, we were doing publicity, or dissecting past performances. It was always something.

But for these beautiful women, I'd squeeze something in somewhere. Which gave me an idea. I'd have to think about that more later.

I glanced over to see Oaklyn looking down at her hands, which she held in her lap. She was hunched forward slightly, like the weight of everything was starting to descend on her and push her down, bit by bit.

I got it. One minute, she was living her life, keeping me at arm's length. The next minute, she was faking an engagement to me and trying to make a home for her sister. I thought about telling her to call Kymmie and admit we weren't engaged, but that might do irreparable damage to our case. To her case.

I had to remind myself Cadence was Oaklyn's sister. I cared about Oaklyn a lot, but at the end of the day I wasn't her fiancé. I wasn't even her boyfriend. I wasn't Cadence's father. I was just a fuckboy hockey player who was falling head over heels for a woman who made it clear we were only friends.

Fine, I could be her friend, but I'd be the best friend she ever had. Until she realized we could both have so much more.

Until she realized I was right, she was mine. Then the ring would be real.

Chapter Fifteen

Oaklyn

"Well, this is swanky." Gran pronounced it 'swaan-kaay.' Eyes huge, she looked around Nate's guest house, taking in everything.

"So, you'll move in with Cadence and me?" I asked carefully.

"Absolutely not," she said. "I like my independence. Besides, you lovebirds don't want me here, cramping your style." She nodded as though that was that, her earrings swinging back and forth.

"We talked about this," I said. "I like having you around, and you'd have your own space here. It's totally separate from the main house."

"Maybe that's the problem. Did you ever think of that, hmmm?" She placed her hands on her hips and cocked her head like she was a sassy twelve year old.

One of her earrings hit her in the side of the face and sat there, looking back at me. "Maybe I want to be in the main house."

"There's plenty of rooms in there if you want to," I said, with as much patience as I could summon. Right now, that wasn't very much. "I'm sure Nate can find you one with your own bathroom."

She straightened her head, the earring sliding free. "That would be even closer to you and your naked, sweaty sexy time." She pointed a finger at me. "Not that there's anything wrong with naked, sweaty sexy time, but I don't want to witness it."

I wanted to tell her there would be no naked, sweaty sexy time. Not even when my clit very much wanted to come out and play.

I couldn't tell her the engagement was fake either. Without doubt, she'd blurt it out at the worst possible moment. Probably when Kymmie was inspecting the property. Once everything was sorted out, we'd tell her the truth. She'd laugh her ass off. At least one of us would find it amusing.

I rolled the heel of my hand back and forth across my forehead. "I worry about you living by yourself, but this isn't just about you or me. We're trying to provide a stable home life for Cadence."

"I fail to see what that has to do with me," she

said stubbornly. "She's your sister. Your father's daughter. I asked you once to think about what your mother would say when she finds out Cadence is here. Have you thought about that?"

I should have known she hadn't let go of that bone. She was like a dog, gnawing at it, growling if anyone got too close.

"I have thought about it," I said evenly. "And I decided my mother is a grown woman. I know what my father did hurt her. It hurt me too. But you know what, it hurt Cadence as well. When it comes down to it, she's the only one here who's completely innocent."

"How do you see that?" Gran asked. "If you're trying to suggest I did anything to drive your mother and father apart..."

"Of course not," I said. Trying not to lose my shit, I took a few steps over to the window to look out at the garden. A stone wall separated the property from the street. This place would give my grandmother all the privacy she needed, if only she'd let me help her. After a moment, I turned back.

"What I'm saying is that we're the adults here. We're the ones who can decide to let go of the past and stop letting it drag us down. You and I, we didn't ask for any of this, but neither did Cadence. She's the one who matters here. And also..." I hesitated. "I might have told social services that you're living here and helping us take care of her. That might help sway their decision one way or the other."

"Oaklyn Jane Walsh, you know that's emotional blackmail, right?" she asked.

I thought she'd be annoyed, but she seemed impressed.

"I learned from the best," I told her. "Don't tell me you wouldn't prefer to be up here in Hardball Ridge, with a view of the ocean outside the front gate." The main house had one and it was incredible. From the kitchen window, you could see all the way across the city, and down to the bay.

"I'll think about it," she said. "But if I stay here, it'll be temporary. Just until social services get their shit together. Then I'll be back at my place, living my best life. Although, I gotta admit, the slope of the roads here are perfect for skateboarding."

I suppressed a groan. "Please don't skateboard down the roads. Or anywhere else, for that matter. Have you forgotten what happened the last time?"

She held her hands up in front of her, a smile on the corners of her mouth. "I remember... A big surge of adrenaline. The wind in my hair. The rush of speed."

"The broken wrist," I said. "Me having to move to Lowball Bay to take care of you."

"Me not needing it," she said tartly. "I was doing fine without your help."

"You couldn't carry a pot of pasta over to the sink to drain it," I reminded her. "It's okay to need help. It happens to all of us from time to time. Even the invincible Henrietta Henstridge."

She huffed. "I would have figured something out. I was perfectly capable of spooning the pasta out of the water, bit by bit."

"Of course you are, I was—"

I was interrupted by Nate sticking his head in through the doorway and grinning at us. It totally wasn't his smile that made my heart skip a beat. No way.

"You look at home here already," he told Gran. "You're welcome to redecorate if you want. It's a bit impersonal."

"It's neutral as fuck," Gran declared. "I've never seen so many shades of beige before. Whoever decorated it should be ashamed of themselves." She clicked her tongue as though the walls and carpet were all bright pink, or in clashing shades, offensive to the eye. Or worse still, so modern the place was stark. Yes, it was beige, but it was cozy and comfortable. I'd lived in worse places.

Nate glanced around like he hadn't taken the time to have a good look before. "You're right, it is beige. The place could use some color, but that's what you're here for. To liven it up."

"Bullshit," Gran said. "I'm here because Oaklyn thinks I need a babysitter. I've been looking after myself for longer than you've been alive."

"Of course you have," Nate said. "But you don't strike me as the kind of person who likes spending a bunch of time alone. You like having people around, right?"

She opened and closed her mouth a couple of times before finally saying, "I guess you could say that." She gave the impression she would have preferred to have teeth pulled then to make an admission like that, but he wasn't wrong. She was the quintessential social butterfly if I ever met one. Her house was cute, and her independence was important, but she was happier in a crowd than she was alone, with her own company. Up here on the ridge, she'd be surrounded by people her own age. And, of course, us.

"Then it's perfect," he concluded. "You have your space, but you can hang out with us whenever you want." As an additional enticement, he said, "I have a lot of the team around for parties and stuff like that. I could introduce you to the head coach. He's about the same age as you, maybe a little younger."

Gran grunted. "I was about to say, what makes you think I want a man my age? If a younger man is good enough for my granddaughter, it's good enough for me."

Nate stepped over and put an arm around me. "I hope to be good enough for Oaklyn. She deserves someone amazing. Right, cupcake?"

"Right, honeybun," I said with slightly less enthusiasm. I hated lying to my grandmother. Or my sister. Or the rest of the world.

Nate was a high-profile player. It was only a matter of time until word of our engagement got out. If it hadn't already. When everyone found out the truth, they were going to hate me. They'd probably suggest I was using him. Although, I was, wasn't I? Cadence wasn't his sister. Gran wasn't his grandmother. But he was here, stuck in a fake engagement because of me.

The sooner everyone knew the truth, the better.

"Of course she does, she's my granddaughter," Gran said. "She comes from a long line of awesome women. Some make better choices than others." She didn't need to explain she was referring to my mother. It was even more obvious than her massive earrings, or her bright orange bucket hat. No one would ever describe my grandmother as subtle. More like all up in your face, all the time.

I liked that about her, but sometimes it was a lot.

"Does that mean you think Oaklyn made a good choice?" Nate asked. He seemed sincerely hopeful that she'd say he was perfect for me.

I glanced at him to remind him this wasn't real. It couldn't be real. He deserved better than me. He deserved someone who could give him everything without holding anything back. Without being scared she was going to make an absolute mess of things. Someone who wasn't already thinking about leaving town and not looking back.

"Let me see," Gran said slowly. "Young, good-looking, athletic, a few bucks in the bank."

"Smart, charming," Nate added. "Devoted to Oaklyn."

The smile he gave me was so soft that, for a moment, I almost believed this was real. That he loved me and wanted to spend the rest of his life with me. That he meant it when he said I was his.

"You can join in any minute," Gran told me. "In

fact, go for it. What do you like the most about your fiancé? Is it his big cock?"

My face heated. "Gran!"

She chuckled, amused that she got a response from me.

"That's just an added bonus," Nate said. "Right, cupcake? Don't be shy though, tell your grandmother what you like the most about me."

He and I were going to have words after this. It wasn't fair to put me on the spot, especially in front of Gran. If we were going to convince people, then we'd have to start with her. If she wasn't fooled, then no one else would be.

"I like your sense of humor," I told him. "And the way you don't let anyone hold you back. You know what you want and you go after it."

"Yes I do," he said. "You certainly made me work hard." He leaned over to whisper in my ear, "And you make me hard."

Now all I could think about was his cock, erect and ready for me. Thick and proud.

He knew exactly what I was thinking, I saw that on his face. Pleased, with a hint of smug. He wanted to get to me as much as he could. While he could.

"I'll keep making you work hard," I said.

"Wouldn't want you to get complacent and start taking me for granted."

"Translation, don't be a cheating prick like her father," Gran said. "If you do, I'll personally cut off that cock of yours." She made a slicing motion through the air, before tossing his invisible, dismembered cock over her shoulder.

Nate's hand dropped to the front of his groin. "I'd never cheat on Oaklyn. I can promise you that. She's not like anyone I've ever met before. I didn't believe in love at first sight until I saw her. But now I do, because it happened to me. To both of us, right cupcake?"

"It might have taken me a bit longer, honeybun," I said. I wasn't going to make this that easy on him.

"But you got there in the end," he said. "Now, do you have enough boxes to pack all your things into?"

Chapter Sixteen

Nate

"You're what?" Blake laughed so hard he doubled over. He slid into the splits before falling onto his back and kicking his padded legs in the air.

"Not that funny." I leaned on my stick and looked down at him.

"Not that funny, he says!" He laughed even harder.

"Is there a problem?" Coach Lampton skated over to us, hands by his sides. He was a professional hockey player back in his day. If there was anything about ice hockey he didn't know, it wasn't worth knowing.

"Yeah, Nate has lost his mind, Coach," Blake said. He rolled over onto his knees, leaning his weight on his catcher.

"I was going to say the same about Blake," I said. "You might want to consider a replacement for Friday night's game."

Blake flipped me off with a gloved finger. "There's nothing wrong with me. Tell Coach what you just said. He looked like he could use a good laugh."

Coach's gaze slid to me. "Southwell?"

By now, a group of players surrounded us, all coming to see what the fuss was about.

Cam and Flynn both looked like they didn't know which of us was crazier. Knowing them, their money was on both of us.

I muttered something under my breath.

"What was that?" Coach asked.

"I said I'm engaged," I said louder.

"As in busy?" Cam asked. "Or enjoying training?"

"As in to-be-married," I snapped. "I'm engaged to be married, okay?" I started to skate away, but Flynn grabbed my wrist and held me there.

"Since when?" he asked, his voice as even and steady as ever.

"With who?" Blake asked, barely containing another hoot of laughter. "Is it one of the Casey twins? Wait, is it both of them? Is that even legal anywhere in this country yet?"

"I'm not engaged to either of the fucking Casey twins," I snarled. "And I'm not engaged to some puck bunny I met last night either." It wouldn't have taken long for someone to suggest that. Probably Blake.

"Of course not," Flynn said. "We're happy for you. Right?" He looked around at everyone through his visor, blue eyes full of intent.

"Absolutely," Cam said. "I'm sure you and... Oaklyn will be happy together. I hope you're as happy as Andi and me." He seemed sincere, as did Flynn. Blake didn't seem able to stop laughing.

"Yes, yes, that's good," Coach said. "Congratulations. Maybe you can get your head back in the game now." He seemed particularly unimpressed. Not with my announcement, but with the distraction.

"Sorry, Coach." Stick in hand, I skated back to the blue line.

"She must not know you very well," Zack said. "Maybe I should tell her what you're really like. She'll probably run a fucking mile." He'd followed me across the ice. "Better yet, she might prefer me."

"What's your problem, Reed?" I asked. "Maybe you need to get laid once in a while."

"Is that the best you got?" he asked derisively. "Some of us don't spend their entire lives thinking with our cock."

"What do you think with then?" I asked. "I haven't seen any proof you have a brain."

He rolled his eyes. "You're a motherfucker, Southwell. And you need to work on your insult game. Yours are straight out of grade school."

If that was how he wanted to play it, then I'd play along. I stuck my tongue out at him and said, "It takes one to know one."

"Cockhead." He turned to head toward the centre of the ice.

"I know you are, but what am I?" I called out after his back.

He flipped me off over his shoulder.

"Don't rise to his bait," Flynn advised, taking his place in the centre.

"I'm over everyone throwing out bait" I said. I glanced back at Blake, who was back on his feet, dancing a jig in front of the goal.

"Do you love her?" Flynn asked. "Because if you ask me anything, that's all that matters. The rest is just white noise."

I breathed out hard enough to mist the front of

my visor. He was right. I shouldn't let them get to me. The only thing that mattered was that I loved Oaklyn.

Wait.

Love? Had I really thought that? Yes, I had and I knew it was true. I'd fallen in love with her the moment I saw her. The more I got to know her, the deeper I fell. She was it for me. I'd never feel this way about another person as long as I lived.

Her, Cadence, even Gran, they were my family now.

"You got it bad, don't you?" Flynn asked.

Clearly he hadn't expected to see the day when Nathaniel Southwell fell in love with something other than hockey. To be honest, neither had I. No wonder Blake laughed so hard. I looked forward to the day I could laugh at him for the same reason. If any woman could tame the energetic goalie, that was. She'd have her work cut out for her.

"Real bad," I said with a grin.

"Yeah." Now Flynn looked distracted.

I followed his gaze to where Valentina stood beside the ice, talking to the strength and conditioning coach.

"She's pretty," I said.

He cut me a look. "She shouldn't be here." Before I could respond he added, "We should be focusing." He turned to his alternate, ready for the coach to drop the puck and start the practice game.

I frowned at him. The last person I expected to object to having a woman coaching us was him. Even Zack seemed to have more respect than Flynn. Not that he was disrespectful to her face. At least, not that I'd seen. He was just...quietly hostile.

Whatever his problem was, I hoped he'd get over it.

I gripped my stick and got ready for play to start.

"Southwell, a word," Coach said as I was stepping off the ice behind the others.

I stopped just inside the gate, so suddenly one of the other players almost ran into the back of me. In turn, I almost ran into Cam, who stopped just as quickly.

When Coach spoke, we all listened. Even if it wasn't directed at us.

"Ohhh, Southwell is in trouble," Blake teased. He pulled his gloves off and waved them in the air beside his face like a pom-pom.

"Grow up, Eastwood," I told him.

He lowered his hand and tipped his head to the side. "After careful consideration, I decided to decline your suggestion. Thank you for your input." He pulled off his mask and helmet and grinned, white teeth contrasting against his dark beard.

"Get going, Eastwood," Coach told him. He waved him away, then everyone else.

"Ohhh, now Eastwood is in trouble," Cam teased. He offered Flynn a fist bump, which the center wisely ignored. Instead, he gave Cam a shove towards the locker room.

Coach gave him a glance that was purely unamused. "Don't think I won't bench your ass, North."

"Sorry, Coach," Cam said, not looking sorry, even though he knew full well his relationship with Andi wouldn't stop him from being reprimanded. Here on the ice, Coach Lampton was the boss. Andi wouldn't interfere with him exercising his authority. Cam would get no sympathy from her. Not in public anyway.

In private— Yeah, I didn't want to mentally go there either. Cam was a friend and and Andi was fucking adorable, but I didn't want to imagine their sex life. Or any of the other guys for that matter. Especially Zack, now that I thought about it.

Although, if I'm honest, I was pretty sure his sex life involved his right hand. No wonder he was so uptight all the time. If he loosened up, he might even make friends with other guys on the team. He had to have some redeeming qualities, I just didn't know what they were.

"What's up, Coach?" I pulled off my gloves and helmet and held them under my arm.

"Your relationship with Ms. Walsh," Coach said.

"If you're about to say she works here, so does Andi," I said quickly.

Since there was a precedent for workplace relationships at the Sea Dragons, he couldn't tell us to stop seeing each other. Not while Cam and Andi were practically married. Could he? He'd be hypocritical if he did. Although, the team's owner got away with more than a regular player would.

"We can keep it professional. I mean, we already do." Sort of. Except me skipping practice to help her with Cadence. He was less than impressed with me for that.

"That wasn't what I was going to say," he said. "But if your relationship interferes with your job, then we'll have something to discuss. What I wanted to talk to you about was, have you announced your engagement anywhere outside of here?" He gestured around the rink.

"Not formally," I said. "We haven't gotten that far yet. This is all so new."

He nodded shortly. "Good. Make an appointment to speak to Alice North and work out how to break this to social media. We want to control the narrative here, not let people speculate on the situation."

I tightened my grip on my helmet. He had a point. If this leaked out without us controlling it, people would say all sorts of stupid things about Oaklyn. I didn't want any wannabe puck bunnies coming after her because they thought I belonged to them in some way. There was only one person I belonged to, and that was her. We had to make that very clear, and to do that we had to step carefully.

Not to mention what a media circus might do to Cadence and us getting her settled here in Lowball Bay. Something like that might damage her permanently. The kid had it rough enough for the last while without me adding to it, however inadvertently.

"That's a good idea, Coach," I said. "We'll keep it

all under wraps until Alice can figure out the best way for us to make the announcement."

"I have one of those every now and again." He clapped me on the back. "Don't screw this up, Southwell. I've met Oaklyn; she seems like a nice girl."

"She is nice," I said. "She's incredible. You're not going to tell me she deserves better than a reformed fuckboy, are you?" If he was, I was going to walk away right now. That got old so long ago it predated the dinosaurs at this point.

"That's up to you and her to decide," he said. "If she loves you, then I'm happy for you." He nodded and moved away to talk to the other coaches.

He'd never been big on talking about our personal lives or passing judgment. He was here for one reason and one reason only—to coach hockey. To mold us into the best team we could be.

I wouldn't say he had a one track mind, but he was a freight train hurtling in a single direction. Toward the Stanley Cup.

That was one more reason to respect the man. He didn't insert himself into other people's business, and he was passionate about the team. What else could anyone want in a head coach?

I started toward the locker room, his words

echoing in my brain. *If she loves you.* Did she love me? Could she love me?

Yes, I knew she could, she just had to let herself. And she would. I had a few ideas that would help, but first I needed to make that appointment with Alice. The sooner we made this official, the better.

I had a few ideas about how we could do that. Ones Oaklyn would never forget.

Chapter Seventeen

Oaklyn

"Are you sure about this?" I glanced over at Nate, who walked beside me. The spring in his step suggested he was just fine with everything. Like always, it was me who had doubts.

He took my hand and closed the distance between us. "I'm very sure. Also, this is Coach's orders anyway. Who am I to disobey him?"

I snorted. "Who are you trying to kid? I never would have picked you for a Boy Scout."

"I'm not," he agreed. "But there are things you ignore and things you don't. This falls into the things you don't category. Alice is the best at what she does. She'll figure out the best way to handle the situation. So to speak."

He grinned at his own choice of words. While I tried hard not to think about handling him.

This is temporary, I reminded myself. Just for a couple of weeks. Maybe a month. Then we'd go back to normal and live our separate lives. It might be a good idea for me to think about moving on sooner than I planned. A clean break would be better for both of us. Gran could be her legal guardian. They could watch out for each other. They'd clash once in a while, but this could be just what they both needed.

If that was true, then why did the idea hurt so much?

"I guess you guys face scrutiny on the daily?" I asked. "That must get old pretty quick."

"It comes with the territory," he said easily. "I'd rather play hockey and be scrutinised than not play hockey at all."

"Was this all you've ever wanted to do?" I asked. "Become a professional hockey player? With every-thing that goes along with that." Yes, I did mean puck bunnies, but also the money and fame.

"Growing up, I wanted to be an engineer," he said. "I had the grades, but not the money. I applied for a scholarship based on being able to play hockey, but it turned out I was good enough to go pro. So I did and never really looked back."

"But you looked back a little bit?" I asked.

We stopped at the bank of elevators a few feet from the staff gym. Nate pressed the up button. Then pressed it again, because the elevators in the arena were known for being finicky. They were on the list to be looked at in the off-season. When the arena wasn't quite as busy.

"Sometimes I wonder what it would have been like if I stayed at college," he said. "I could have been working on the next environmentally friendly car as we speak. To be honest, I probably would have ended up working for my brother. Which would have had its ups and downs."

"You don't get along?" I asked.

"We're both ambitious," he said slowly. "I would have wanted to tell him how to run his business and he would have... Let's say he wouldn't appreciate it. We're a lot alike, I guess. It's probably better this way. I get to be the cool uncle instead of a thorn in his side."

"I'm sure you'd never be a thorn in his side," I said. "You might have been the perfect team."

"I think he already had that," Nate said softly. "He

married the woman of his dreams and had a beautiful family with her. Natalie made him happier than I've ever seen him. When she died, he was gutted. If it wasn't for the girls, I don't know how he'd go on."

"That must be hard," I said. "It sucks when you have everything you want and it's torn away from you. And you wonder if there was something you could have done or said that would have stopped it. Maybe just...the right word at the right time. Something."

Nate drew me to a stop. He looked down at me, brow creased, eyes full of worry.

"You know what your father did wasn't your fault, right?" His tone was firm, but gentle at the same time. "He did it because he wanted to. Not because of anything you said or did. Not because of anything you didn't do or say either."

I averted my gaze. "I know that, but I..."

"You still blame yourself," he finished for me.

"Why weren't Mom and I enough?" I asked. "I tried to be the best person I could be. I thought if I did, maybe he'd come back. I worked hard at school. I don't curse. I didn't..." I shook my head. "It wasn't enough."

"For someone like him, nothing would be enough," Nate said. "You're the sweetest, smartest, most beautiful woman I ever met and he's an idiot for missing out on seeing you grow up."

I blinked through a haze of tears. "I hate myself for thinking any of this," I whispered. "Because if he came back, Cadence would have missed out. That wouldn't have been fair to her."

"The whole situation was unfair to both of you," he insisted. "What he did to you and both of your mothers was a dick move. He couldn't keep it in his pants and ended up hurting two families."

Nate reared back slightly. "Is that why you won't let yourself go with me? Because you think I'll do the same thing to you?" He looked genuinely hurt.

I looked down at the worn, linoleum floor. Scuffed from thousands of passing feet.

"Some people never want to be tied down," I whispered.

He sucked in a harsh breath. "We should talk to Alice. We'll talk about the rest of this later." To punctuate his words, the elevator doors slid open and dinged happily. A direct contrast to the current mood between us.

"Nate—" I sighed and followed him into the elevator. He hadn't let my hand go and didn't while we traveled in silence up to the third floor and into the management section of the Sea Dragons Arena.

"Alice's office is this way." He gestured. "She's expecting us." He glanced at a clock on the wall as we walked past. "She'll be surprised we're on time."

"Are you known for being late, Mr. Defenseman?" I asked, wanting to lighten the mood.

The glance he gave was almost back to his normal, lighthearted self. The hurt was still there, but he was fighting to push it aside.

"I'm known for coming when I'm ready," he said with a slanted grin.

I did my best to ignore the way my heart flipped at his smile and yet another innuendo I walked right into. I was going to have to start looking where I was going. Physically and verbally, because I narrowly missed walking into the door frame of Alice's office.

I could totally blame my distraction on holding hands with the most attractive man in the NHL. That would distract any girl. Hard as I tried, I wasn't immune to him or his charms. If I thought anything could come of this, I'd happily surrender to them.

"You're late," Alice said as we stepped into the room. She sat behind the desk, dark hair in a neat bob, brown eyes somewhere between irritated and resigned.

"No, we're not," Nate protested. He stopped halfway across the small office. "Shit."

"What is it?" I looked from her to him and back again. Realization gradually dawned, very much unwelcome. "Everyone knows already?"

"I don't know how," Alice admitted. "Someone must have leaked it somehow, probably by accident. Or... Maybe not." She shrugged one shoulder. "Social media has been blowing up for the last hour or so."

She fixed me with a regretful look. "I suggest you don't look. Give it a few days to pass over. I'll organize some things to distract the public and then we can come back together and give an official statement."

I sagged against Nate. "They're saying things about me?" Who would have talked about us? Now I thought about it, the list was longer than it should have been. Starting with Principal George and ending with Gran and Cadence. Letting it slip couldn't have been that difficult. Once it was out, it would have spread like crazy.

And now, it seemed, everyone knew.

"Nate is popular," Alice said. "Sometimes that makes people think things that aren't true. Plenty of people are happy for you though. When I'm done with them, they're going to be ecstatic."

She seemed certain of that. Of course she would,

this was literally her job. Handling public relations and social media. I wondered how many reputations she'd made, or helped to maintain, in her career. No wonder she was frustrated with players like Blake, who seemed determined to push the boundaries of their own reputations as far as they'd go.

"I knew being this awesome was going to bite me on the ass eventually," Nate said. He gripped my hand tighter. "I'm sorry it's biting you in the ass too. I should be the one—" He remembered Alice was sitting right there, closed his mouth and cleared his throat. "We'll talk about that later too."

Alice smirked. "The best thing both of you can do right now is to keep a low profile. I've already spoken to Coach Lampton. He's agreed to let you step away from the team for a few days. As long as you're ready to play on Saturday night."

"You think it'll be sorted by then?" Nate asked. He looked hopeful, but only cautiously optimistic rather than actually optimistic. He would have known better than anyone that stuff like this was unpredictable.

"I think ice hockey waits for no man," she said. "I can only promise to do the best I can to turn this around." She made a turning motion in the air with her finger. "Social media is fickle. Give them a day or two and they'll be talking about the goalie from Seattle who's retiring after so many years. Everyone loves him."

"I was thinking about leaving town for a couple of days," Nate said. "Getting Oaklyn and her sister out of the city."

I stared at him. That was news to me. How long had he been thinking about that? I got the impression it wasn't a spur of the moment thing. Where did he want to take us?

Evidently we had quite a bit of talking left to do. Unless he decided to end it because I made the comparison between him and my father. Honestly, I wasn't sure if I would blame him if he did. No one wanted to be compared to an asshole, even if there were some noticeable parallels between them.

At the end of the day, it amounted to the same thing. I wasn't going to try to tie down anyone who didn't want to commit.

"That might be a good idea," Alice agreed. "Have a breather. By the time you get back, people won't remember who Nate Southwell even is."

"Hey!" he protested playfully. "I like to think I'm not that forgettable."

She smiled. To me she said, "Hockey players and their egos. I get them every time."

"I'd flip you off, but I don't want to offend my fiancée," Nate said with a sniff.

"You should probably not flip off the woman who's trying to help us," I said.

It wasn't lost on me that she might not need to help us if it wasn't for his reputation. That might be something we couldn't get past.

"I knew I liked you," Alice said. "We should go for drinks some time, if you're game?"

"I'd like that," I said.

I hadn't made many friends in Lowball Bay. I never did. Why make friends when you had no intention of staying? Leaving again just hurt everyone involved. Or maybe it just hurt me. My fear of getting attached to anyone followed me for the last sixteen years.

Maybe it was time to start trying to put it aside.

But what if I did and it led to me having my heart ripped out of my chest and stomped on?

Chapter Eighteen

Nate

"Where are we going?" Cadence looked at me doubtfully.

"You'll see when we get there," I said. "Pack enough for a couple of days away, but pack warm."

Her minute eye roll was clearly intended to remind me she was from a place with a similar climate to Lowball Bay. Temperature wise, that was. It didn't rain here as much as it did in Seattle.

"That's a good question though." Gran stood in the doorway to Cadence's room. "Where are you going?"

I turned and offered her one of my best grins. "I'm not telling you either. Will you be all right here by yourself?" Oaklyn wasn't comfortable leaving her, but Gran was safer here than in her old house.

Gran waved dismissively. "I'll be fine. I have a hot date with the guy next door. In fact, it's best if you're not around. I can get loud, if you know what I mean." She tried to wink, but ended up closing her eyes and squeezing them shut.

"Gran!" Cadence grimaced. "TMI."

Gran shook her finger at Cadence. "Just wait till you get to my age, girl. You'll realize there's nothing to be ashamed of. Quite the opposite, in fact. Orgasms are good for stress relief." She squinted at me. "Doesn't seem to be working for Oaklyn."

Was she accusing me of not giving Oaklyn enough orgasms? Yes. Yes, she was. I couldn't exactly tell her I wasn't giving her granddaughter any orgasms. Not yet, that was. Hopefully this trip away would make her see how I felt about her. When she did, I'd give her all the orgasms she could handle. And then some.

"She's under a lot of pressure right now," I said evenly. "Don't worry, I'll take good care of her."

"Atta boy." Gran nudged my side with her elbow. "I knew there was a reason I liked you."

"I thought it was my good looks and charm," I said.

"That too." She nodded so vigorously, her

earrings hit her in the side of the face. Those things should come with a hazard warning.

"If you want me to pack, can you stop being icky?" Cadence asked. "No one needs to hear about your sex lives. Especially me." She pulled her backpack out from under the bed and opened the zipper.

I made a mental note to buy her a new one. This one had clearly seen better days. Hell, it looked like it had seen better *years*.

"We'll leave you to it." I stepped out of her room, herding Gran in front of me. When we were far enough away so Cadence couldn't overhear, I said, "Do you think she's okay?"

"That depends which she you're referring to," Gran said. "Cadence seems more or less fine, for a moody teenager. Oaklyn, on the other hand..."

I stopped and lowered my voice further. "You think Oaklyn isn't okay?"

"Like you said, she's under a lot of pressure," Gran said.

She was more serious than I'd seen her before, so she had my attention.

"If you ask me, the girl doesn't know what she wants. Or if she does, she won't let herself have it. What her asshole father did to her mother, it really did a number on the kid. She'd like a butterfly, flitting from one flower to another, never settling on one." She laced her fingers together and steepled her pointer fingers before pointing them at me.

"Until you came along. You might be the best thing to have ever happened to my granddaughter. But if you hurt her, I'll snip your dick off with a pair of scissors and feed it to a goat."

That was disturbingly specific.

"You have a goat?" I asked.

She waved her fingers at me. "I'll find one. Someone in Lowball Bay must have one somewhere. Or a pig. I hear they're good at disposing of bits of people."

"I'll bear that in mind," I assured her. "I have no intention of hurting Oaklyn."

It was nice to know Gran thought Oaklyn would settle down for me. Would she though, or was she planning to be out of here the moment we ended our fake engagement? I was going to have to pull out all the stops to make her want to stay. I wasn't going to let her walk out of my life.

"I know you don't, but shit happens," Gran said. "I've spent the last sixteen years helping pick up the pieces of what he did to Caroline. My daughter was head over heels for that man until she discovered what he'd done." Her eyes glazed as she thought back.

"He broke more than her heart. He broke her. He irreparably damaged her relationship with Oaklyn. Her self-esteem was in the toilet. The cheating was enough, without knocking up another woman."

I thought back to the conversation I had with Oaklyn outside the elevator. The way she suggested my being a player in a past life must mean I was a prime candidate for doing the same crappy thing to her. I won't lie, it stung.

At the same time, I understood where she was coming from. Her father was a player too. One who must have convinced her mother he'd stick with her life. The difference between him and me was that I meant it. I had no interest in any other woman. I knew I wouldn't, not ever again.

How the hell did I convince Oaklyn of that?

"I'm sorry for what he put both of them through," I said. "I'm sure Caroline is amazing. Her mother and her daughter both are. She didn't deserve to be treated like that."

"Who does?" Gran asked.

"I'd put forward the name of Zack Reed, but I don't even think he deserves to be treated like that," I said. I hadn't given up on the possibility there might be a decent guy in there somewhere. Deep down. Deep, deep down. In a place so deep he might not even know it was there.

"No one deserves it," she said.

"But she's okay now?" I asked. "Caroline, I mean. Oaklyn mentioned she remarried."

"Yeah, she finally found herself a decent man," Gran said. "Robert also knows which of his bits a goat will get if he hurts her, but she's happy." She glanced back in the direction of Cadence's room. "For now."

"You really think she's going to have a problem with Cadence being here?" I asked.

"I think it's going to dredge up some old shit," Gran said.

"Then we'll deal with it," I said. "In the meantime, I better round up my womenfolk and hit the road."

"I'm ready." Cadence appeared, backpack on her back, phone in her hand.

She appeared so suddenly I wondered how much of the conversation she overheard. I got nothing from her expression apart from the usual barrier she put between herself and the rest of the world.

"Great," I said as cheerfully as I could manage. "Let's go and find your sister and see if she's ready."

"She's probably deciding which of her yoga pants to pack," Gran said. "And picking out her prettiest underwear for your enjoyment."

"Ewww," Cadence complained.

I didn't try to correct her. There was nothing more compelling than the idea of Oaklyn in pretty underwear. Except the idea of her out of it.

I needed to stop this train of thought before I got a raging hard on in front of her grandmother and sister. It was too early in the day for that kind of embarrassment.

Gran cackled. "Enjoy your family bonding time. Don't forget to take Monopoly with you."

Cadence stood stock still, her arms crossed over her chest. "If you bring that stupid game, I'm not going."

"We won't bring Monopoly," I assured her.

"No board games," she insisted.

I held up my hands in surrender. "No board games. Promise. Why don't you go down to the garage and put your stuff in the car? The SUV that is. The Maserati's a tight fit for three people."

Cadence gave me a doubtful look, but headed for the stairs that led down to the garage.

"What kind of card game are you taking?" Gran asked.

I grinned. "There's no pulling the wool over your eyes, is there?"

"No siree-bob," she agreed. "Go on, fess up. It's Cards Against Humanity, isn't it? If it isn't, I'm going to be disappointed in you." She cocked her head. "Unless it's something like Cards Against Hockey. Then I'm here for it."

"I'd tell you, but then Oaklyn or Cadence might overhear," I said. "I guess you're going to have to find out from them when we get back."

She huffed. "Fine, I'll wait. But I want all the details. Unless you play strip poker. In which case, I only want about three quarters of the details."

"That game isn't very family friendly," I pointed out.

"That's why you play it after everyone else has gone to bed," Gran said. "In case you hadn't noticed, I wasn't born yesterday. Or even the day before."

"You must have been wild back in the day," I said.

She grinned, showing a bunch of gum above and below her white teeth. "Boy, you have no idea. If it wasn't for Oaklyn, I would happily have shown you."

"If I met you first, I might have let you," I said. What was a forty-four year age gap anyway?

"You missed out in this life," she said. "Maybe in the next one. On the other hand, I have a feeling you're meant for Oaklyn in the next life too." She patted me on the arm and wandered away towards the kitchen, whistling under her breath.

She might be right about that. In the meantime, I had my work cut out trying to convince Oaklyn I was meant for her in *this* life.

Chapter Nineteen

Oaklyn

"We're going to Highball Creek?" I peered out the window at the sign we passed. I should have guessed when we got onto the Golong Highway. This was the quickest route there.

Although, if you kept on driving, you'd end up in Canada. That wouldn't have been so bad. On the other hand, I'd heard a lot about Highball Creek, but I'd never been there.

"Isn't that the middle of bumfuck nowhere?" Cadence asked from the back seat. She sounded underwhelmed.

Okay, what else was new? She didn't seem to be settling in the way I hoped she would. Granted, it had only been a few days. I shouldn't expect miracles.

"That's the best thing about it," Nate said. He glanced over at me and grinned. If he didn't stop giving me those panty melting smiles, I was going to be in trouble.

"That it's in bumfuck nowhere?" I asked.

"Exactly," he said. "Half the time, you can't even get cellphone reception, and the last time I was there, the Internet was slower than snail mail."

Cadence groaned.

"Give it a chance," Nate said over his shoulder. "There's good people in Highball."

"Says you," she said half under her breath, but she fell silent after that, her eyes on her phone. Occasionally grooving to the music coming through her earbuds.

"Somewhere without cell and Internet service sounds wonderful," I said.

Maybe I could convince him to leave me there and they could go back to the city and live their lives. Even a small town could use a personal trainer, right? Or I could start over, doing something new. I didn't know what, but that was part of the fun. Getting to know a new place and new skills. Putting old judgements behind me.

"It's perfect for a couple of days," Nate said. "I

don't think I could live my whole life in a map dot. Everyone knowing my business. Gossiping about me. Gossiping about everyone else."

"How is that different from Lowball Bay?" I asked.

Nate smiled and slowed the car at the turn off to Highball Creek. "It's easier to tell people to fuck off face-to-face. If you do that on the Internet, someone will take a screenshot and share it around."

"I can tell people to fuck off if I want to?" Cadence asked.

"No, you can't," I said. "There are nicer ways of telling people to go away. And watch your language."

She huffed in disappointment. "Gran would say—"

I twisted around to look at her. "Gran is a terrible role model."

"At least she enjoys her life," Cadence said meaningfully.

"Who says I don't enjoy my life?" I asked.

I probably earned the eye roll she gave me before she looked back at her phone. I sat around again and looked over to Nate.

"Am I that bad? I mean, I get job satisfaction. I play board games with my grandmother when she wants me to. I..." I couldn't think of another thing I did that was fun.

"You could let your hair down a little," Nate said. "But it's okay if you don't want to. Not everyone can be like Gran. Maybe you're meant to be the anti-Gran."

"That sounds like the person no one invites to parties or wants to spend any time with," I said, ending the sentence with a sigh.

"I want to spend time with you," he said. "So does Cadence. Right, Cadence?"

Either she was ignoring him or her music was too loud, because she kept her eyes on her phone, her shoulders swaying back and forth.

"She really does," Nate assured me. "She's going to have a blast. And so are you. It'll be so much fun, it'll blow your mind." He grinned as he said the word blow, but evidently decided not to point it out in front of the teenager.

I tried not to picture what it would be like to be on my knees in front of him, taking him into my mouth. Tasting him. Sucking until he groaned and shattered. My clit pulsed.

This is fake, I reminded myself. Temporary. What was important was that Cadence bonded with him and Gran. Then she'd have choices when I left town. The longer she was with me, the more acutely it felt that I'd be abandoning her when I left. All I wanted was what was best for her. That was the only thing that mattered here. A stable life for my sister. A life I couldn't give her.

We headed down Batters Pitch road until a highway lined with billboards and rest stops gave way to farmland.

A herd of cows barely raised their heads to watch us pass before they returned to nibbling on the grass. Half a mile on, fields lay ready to be planted out for spring. Every now and again, the creek that gave the town its name would appear as a glittering snake winding through the landscape.

"This is beautiful," I said softly. Even before I got out of the car, I felt more at peace than I had in weeks.

"As map dots go, this is my favorite one," Nate said. "I grew up running through those fields over there. Getting muddy from head to toe. That pond over there, we used to play pond hockey."

I peered in the direction he was pointing, to see a frozen over patch of pond among the trees. Barely the size of an ice hockey rink, it would have been perfect to practice on. At the moment it was empty. Of course, it was the middle of the week.

The kids would be doing homework, or chores after school.

"I can see why you like it here," I said as we approached the tiny town. We passed ten or twenty small, mom and pop stores on Main Street before pulling up outside a farmhouse a mile or so out of town. The creek ran behind the house before wandering away through the fields.

"There's nothing here," Cadence said in dismay.

"That's where you're wrong." Nate pushed out of the car and headed around to grab out our bags.

"Nate!" A woman a handful of years older than him, stepped out of the front door of the cottage. She was followed by a couple of kids around Cadence's age, and a couple a few years younger. She hurried over to give him a hug.

"Hey, James." Nate put the bags down on the front porch and hugged her back before holding his hand out to me. "Jamie, this is Oaklyn and her sister, Cadence. Jamie is my favorite sister."

Jamie snorted. "Only sister."

"I said what I said," Nate said. "These are Jamie's kids. Trouble One and Trouble Two." He gestured to the teenagers who gave him eye rolls Gran would have been proud of. "And the little ones are Chip and Munk."

Jamie punched him on the arm. "Don't listen to him. The oldest two are Tessa and Lucy. The twins are Chip and Hank." She pointed to each of them in turn.

Nate grinned. "One out of four ain't bad."

"Mommy says we should call you Uncle Puckhead," Chip declared. He couldn't have been more than about five years old.

Hank giggled. "Uncle Puckhead!"

Tessa and Lucy shared looks.

"They're so cringey," Lucy complained.

"So cringey," Tessa agreed.

"I keep telling them that," Cadence said softly. She looked like she very much wanted to be invited to spend time with them, but was uncertain as to whether they'd accept her or not.

Lucy smiled at her warmly. "Right? Me too. It's like they enjoy being cringey. I'm pretty sure they're doing it on purpose to annoy us."

"That wouldn't surprise me," Tessa said. She was a little slower to smile at Cadence, but after a few moments, it was there, just as warm as her sister's. "Let's get out of here, away from the cringe before it's contagious. Come on, save yourselves." She gestured to Cadence and her sister before heading back into the cottage.

Cadence hesitated.

"We're much cooler than them," Lucy said. She jerked her head towards the door and gave Cadence another genuine smile.

"Go on," Nate said. "My nieces are right, they're much cooler than the rest of us."

"Naw!" Chip said loudly. "I'm the coolest."

"It's too cold out here to talk about who's the coolest," Jamie said. "Let's all get inside where it's warm. Danny is fixing a fire in the fire pit after dinner." She glanced towards the back of the cottage.

"Can we have s'mores?" Hank asked.

"Of course we can." She herded her youngest children inside. "I look forward to getting to know you, Oaklyn. Nate has told me a lot about you. Let me show you to your room."

It was so easy to like her; I hated myself for lying to her as well. That list kept on growing, like a weed after a month of rain. This would all be over soon enough. Hopefully they'd forgive us for the pretence. Or forgive Nate anyway. By then, I'd be gone and forgotten.

We followed Jamie across the hardwood floors and up a set of stairs to the upper floors of the house.

"This is beautiful," I said, running my hand up the banister.

"It's over a hundred years old," Jamie said from the top of the stairs. "It was rundown when we bought the place, but Danny and I renovated it and brought it back to life."

"Danny is a carpenter and general contractor," Nate said. "He could renovate this place with his eyes closed."

"You might be exaggerating slightly," Jamie said with a laugh. She glanced at me and added, "Nate helped with some of the work when he could. He likes to pretend he's not handy, but he actually is. When it suits him to be." She gave her brother a fond, yet slightly scolding look.

Nate shrugged. "If I told any of the guys on the team I knew how to use a hammer or a drill, they'd want me to do all sorts of sh—" He glanced at the boys who trailed us up the stairs. "*Stuff*, in their houses. I wouldn't want to put guys like Danny to shame, or out of work."

Jamie barked a laugh. "Now you're over-exaggerating your skills." She pushed open a timber door that led into a small room at the back of the house.

"A guy can't win," Nate whispered loudly.

"Poor Uncle Puckhead." Chip patted him on the arm and looked sad for him.

I held back a laugh at how adorable he was. If

Nate had children, they might look like Chip and Hank. I had no doubt they'd act like them too. Sassy, with all the answers to everything.

I pushed away the yearning that tried to worm its way into my heart. That was a feeling I'd never know, no matter what happened in the future. I knew that, but the ache would never completely go. It would still linger there when I was old and grey. That one thing I always wanted but could never have.

"Thanks, Chippy." Nate placed our bags down and picked up his nephew. "Can you call me Uncle Nate?"

My ovaries might have exploded then and there if they were able to. Nothing in this world was hotter than a man who was good with children. If anything would make me give in to my insistent clit, it would be this image, right here.

My heart even responded by beating faster a handful of times. I *might* have felt it soften a little, but I probably imagined that.

Chip hummed. "I dunno." He gave an exaggerated shrug.

"Okay, let's try this. Repeat after me. Uncle."

"Uncle," Chip said dutifully.

"Nate," Nate said.

"Nate," Chip echoed.

"Excellent work," Nate said. "Now, put them together. Uncle Nate." He raised a hand in the air to offer Chip the proverbial floor.

Chip grinned. "Uncle Puckhead."

Nate shook his head with mock sadness and placed his nephew back down. "I give up. He's too smart for me."

Jamie grinned. "Story of your life, little brother. Get yourself settled here. We'll see you downstairs for dinner." She waved the boys out and closed the door, leaving us alone in the small bedroom. With one small, double bed.

"I'd offer to sleep on the couch, but there isn't one," Nate said.

That was our sleeping arrangement at his place, but there, he had a huge couch in an alcove to the side of his bedroom. It was almost as big as his bed.

"It's fine," I said. "We're adults, we can manage." After all, we were only going to sleep there, right? Nothing a pair of mature adults couldn't handle.

There wasn't room for a chair in the room, so I sat on the side of the bed. "Your sister is lovely."

"It runs in the family." He sat beside me and placed his hand over mine.

"Along with humility," I remarked.

He grinned. "That too." His smile slowly faded. "Seriously though, she likes you. My sister is an even better judge of character than I am. She knew how awesome you are before she even met you."

"Exactly how much did you tell her about me?" I asked. Lying to her about our engagement was bad enough without him trying to make me sound better than I was.

"Only the good parts," he said. "Mostly about the way you took in Cadence and gave her a home."

"Did I?" I turned to look out the window. From here, I could make out the creek meandering past and a stand of trees beyond that. The only sound was my own heartbeat and the occasional shout from one of the boys downstairs. Everything else here was quiet, still. The opposite of my mind. That was racing as fast as my heart. Faster. Thoughts tumbling over each other, fighting to be seen.

"Of course you did," he assured me. "You didn't send her back to Seattle."

"They didn't want her," I reminded him. "She had nowhere else to go."

I turned back to him. "Thank you for bringing me here. I think it might be exactly what we all need." A few days away from the city to regroup would do us all good. I could forget about social media, and Cadence could enjoy the company of two girls her own age, who seemed to like her already. Not to mention a couple of boys who were clearly as quick as their uncle and just as cheeky.

Nate said something under his breath. It sounded like, "You're all I need."

Chapter Twenty

Nate

"It looks like half of Highball turned out to see their hometown hero," Danny remarked.

"Don't encourage him," Jamie groaned.

I grinned. "It's way too late for that. I was encouraged years ago." I held on tight to Oaklyn's hand and led her down to the fire pit. The flames crackled, reaching towards the sky, hot enough to keep us warm on this otherwise freezing night.

Cadence, Lucy and Tessa sat off to one side, laughing quietly at something on the screen of Lucy's phone. Apparently the cell and Internet services out here got improved at some point. Seeing Cadence smile and connecting with my nieces was more than worth it.

"Well if it isn't Nathanial Southwell." A dark-haired woman sat on a stump by the fire, beer in hand.

"In the flesh," I said.

She looked me up and down and smiled. "So I see. The boss actually gave you some time off?"

I sat down on a stump and pulled Oaklyn down to the one beside me. She reclaimed her hand and placed it in her lap, looking uncomfortable to be here. Every so often, she'd glance in Cadence's direction and her mouth would tighten slightly. Was she unhappy that her sister was making friends? That didn't make sense, but something was clearly getting to her.

"It happens once in a while," I said lightly. "Oaklyn, this is Pia Welling, Andi's sister. And that's Pia's partner." I nodded to the man on the other side of Pia. He nodded back and turned his attention to constructing a s'more.

"Oh." Oaklyn looked surprised. If I wasn't mistaken, slightly relieved as well. I decided I wasn't mistaken, but she pushed it aside so quickly I almost missed it. Was she jealous? Had she thought I was flirting with Pia?

The younger Welling sister was cute and all, but she was Jamie's neighbor, and the boss's sister. Hell, she was practically a sister to me too. It never occurred to me to look at her romantically. Not even short-term. Now she was very much taken and happy, she was well and truly off my radar. Not to mention the fact she wasn't Oaklyn. But if it helped Oaklyn to see me, then that was a bonus.

"It's nice to meet you both," Oaklyn said. "Andi is so lovely. She and Cam are adorable together."

Pia leaned past me to shake Oaklyn's hand. "It's nice to meet you too. It's nice to see my sister settled down with a nice guy."

If Cam himself was here, I'd make some remark about him not being as nice as they might think. Since he wasn't, I decided to let it slide. This time.

Instead I said, "It's nice to see Cam settled with someone nice too." The woman before Andi was a gold digging puck bunny. He deserved better.

Honestly, I never understood what he saw in her. She clearly had bad taste, since she wouldn't give me the time of day. I guess she also pegged me for the kind of guy who'd never settle down, and that wasn't who she had in her sights. She wanted the relationship, and the money and prestige that went with it.

Oaklyn would never be like that. She didn't care about any of the trappings that came with fame. If anything, it made things more difficult. Of course it did, or we wouldn't be here tonight. Fame and money were both a blessing and a curse. Keyboard warriors were the worst kind of troll.

"I hear congratulations are in order." Pia sat back and sipped her beer.

"Yeah." I tried not to stiffen visibly. If she was about to make some dig about past me…

"Congratulations then," she said with a smile. "You might come home to Highball Creek more often? I know your family would like to see more of you. Jamie is always complaining how difficult it is to get you and Rhys to come back and visit. Especially at the same time."

"It's possible," I said carefully. "I'd like to see more of her and the kids too." I slid a glance toward Oaklyn. Stopped to stare at the wistful smile on her face. She was watching Danny help the twins with their s'mores. Danny was smiling and Chip and Hank were giggling over something.

The flames were reflected in her eyes, which shone. I'd never seen the yearning expression on her face, but it was there now. Clear as day. She wanted this. Family. Togetherness. The things she didn't have growing up. The things Cadence didn't have either. It was a shame they hadn't been given the chance to grow up together. Even with so many years between them, it might have made a world of difference.

I leaned over to put my hand on her thigh. "You okay?" I asked softly.

She startled slightly before tearing her eyes away from my nephews and brother-in-law. "I'm fine. Just... Enjoying the moment."

"Are you sure?" Her leg was so warm and firm under my palm I could have kept it there forever. Also, I didn't buy that she was fine. Something was clearly bothering her. "We don't have to stay if you don't want to. This crowd can get a little rowdy."

"Can you call ten people a crowd?" she asked, her tone and expression lighter now, but forced.

"In Highball Creek, this is practically a horde," Pia said. "You should see it in summer though. The population doubles, or triples because of the holiday rentals. People like to escape the city for the mountain air."

"I'm sure it's lovely here in summer," Oaklyn said. "Especially with the creek just there to swim in." She nodded to where it wound past us, flowing slowly like it was in no hurry to reach Lowball Bay and the ocean.

"Some of us swim all year round," I said.

"Only the crazy ones," Pia remarked.

"I never claimed to be sane." I grinned.

"I dare you," Jamie said from the other side of the fire.

I raised an eyebrow at her.

She gave me the same look back. If she was good at anything, it was encouraging me to take chances. She did it all our lives. Sometimes to my detriment, often not.

She was the one who told me I'd be crazy to turn down the opportunity to go pro. I hadn't hesitated long, but it was long enough for her to kick my ass. One of her favorite pastimes was reminding me of that.

In return, I helped her out as often as I could, in as many ways as I could. Including setting up a trust fund for each of the kids. She'd tried to refuse, but I'd done it anyway. She wouldn't say so, but I knew she was grateful.

Still grinning, I rose to my feet.

Oaklyn shot to hers. "You're not really thinking of swimming, are you? It's freezing out."

"I wasn't going to, but Jamie dared me," I said. "Now I kinda have to." I shrugged and started to pull off my hoodie.

"I'm sure you don't have to." Oaklyn looked at Pia, clearly hoping she'd back her up.

"He really does." Pia toasted both of us with her beer. "Welcome to Highball Creek."

"This is crazy," Oaklyn whispered. "I know ice baths are good for you, but..."

"Don't worry about me, I've swam in there a million times." I kissed her cheek and handed her my hoodie. "Keep it warm for me." I slipped off my shoes and socks and headed toward the creek.

"Uncle Nate is going to swim!" Apparently Chip really did know my name. Good for him.

Eager to watch a dumbass doing a dumbass thing, everyone moved away from the fire to follow me down to the creek.

Oaklyn clutched my hoodie like it might serve as a reminder of me if somehow I went under and never resurfaced.

In that moment, I knew she felt the same way about me as I felt about her. Even if she didn't realize it yet.

"Is this where you tell me you take back the dare?" I asked Jamie.

She stood beside me on the edge of the water and grinned. "Little brother, if you're silly enough to jump in there in the middle of winter, I'm not taking anything back." She held up a finger. "However, I will ask that as many people as possible film this on their phones. So we can have a good laugh from a variety of angles."

"Already on it," Lucy said, her phone held up in front of her. Tessa and Cadence stood beside her, both ready.

Cadence actually looked impressed that I'd do something like this. Yes, I was nailing this cool uncle thing. Literally and figuratively.

Likewise, Chip and Hank were jumping up and down and clapping their hands. Excited to see a grown adult doing something they'd probably get into trouble for doing themselves.

I had a feeling I'd be hearing about this for years to come. Would I regret it? Not for a second. Unless...

My gaze slid to my fake fiancée. Right then, this felt anything but fake. She held my hoodie close to her face as though inhaling the scent of me from the fabric. I glanced down at her finger, which was still bare for now. I could easily imagine an engagement ring there, shining bright in the firelight. As soon as we got back to the city, I was taking her shopping.

She looked less worried and more resigned that I was going to do this.

"Can I have a kiss for luck?" I asked. I waited so

long to taste those lips of hers. When would be a better time? I might be about to leap to my doom. Okay, not really, but I wanted to kiss her so much it hurt.

"Do you need luck?" She stepped closer to me. Close enough that our chests were just barely touching. Close enough that I could feel the warmth of her breasts through the fabric of my shirt. I decided I wasn't imagining the hardening of her nipples. And it wasn't just because it was cold out. She wanted me as much as I wanted her. I was tempted to pick her up and carry her back to the cottage, where I'd make love to her slowly but thoroughly. All night long. And all day tomorrow. Until we were both so exhausted we had to take a break.

"Without a doubt," I said. I carefully placed my hand on the back of her head, my fingers in her hair, and slowly lowered my mouth to hers.

The heat of the fire was nothing compared to the way my body ignited as our lips touched. Immediately, I burned from the inside out, wanting to devour her. I tasted her lips. Pushed my tongue between them to taste hers. Savored the little moan that escaped from her while we kissed.

In a heartbeat, I was rock hard, my whole body aching for hers. Needing to touch and be touched.

Her arms went around my neck, pulling me closer still. So close we were almost fused together.

Maybe I didn't need to go for a swim after all. I didn't need to be the cool uncle, not when I had this woman starting to melt right in front of me.

Reluctantly, I started to pull away, but then I was falling. Shoved right off the bank toward the frigid water.

Oaklyn and I were so tangled together, she was falling with me. I tried to keep my feet, but I lost my balance. The bank fell out from under us and we went over.

I let out a shout at the same time as she squealed. We hit the water and went under.

Chapter Twenty-One

Oaklyn

FUCK, IT WAS COLD.

That was my first thought when we hit the water. I kept my hold on Nate until my feet hit the creek bed and I pushed myself back up to the surface.

We popped up at the same time, me gasping for breath, him laughing.

"You pushed me!" he accused, directing the shout to someone back on the bank.

"You were kissing!" Chip and Hank called back simultaneously, then they both giggled..

"You suck." Nate took my hand and we trudged through the water to the edge of the creek, icy water trickling from us.

I was drenched from head to toe, including his

hoodie, which I still had gripped in my fist. The phone in my pocket was probably toast. They could be replaced. This experience couldn't.

"I'm so sorry, Oaklyn," Jamie said. "I didn't know what they were up to until they'd already shoved Nate. I'll have a word with them about pushing people."

She gave them both a look, but was clearly trying not to smile. They might get in trouble, but it wouldn't be too much. I hoped not anyway. Apart from my phone, there was no real harm done.

"Don't listen to a word she says," Nate told me. "My big sister enjoyed it just as much as her kids did. If they hadn't pushed us, she would have. I've always thought she was pure evil, now I have proof. And it's all on video." Water dripping from his hand, he gestured to Cadence and his nieces.

Lucy grinned. "Yeah, and it's gonna go viral." She looked like she was ready to do a happy dance on the spot.

"I don't think it's a good idea to share it with the world," I said.

Nate glanced from Lucy's disappointed face to mine. "I think it's a great idea. What better way to prove to the world we're made for each other?"

"Because your sister's kids pushed us in the creek?" I asked.

"Because they pushed *me* in the creek," he said. "People love that kind of thing. And they'll love the fact that you couldn't let go of me and got pulled in too."

My face heated, which helped with how cold I was. Even stepping close to the fire didn't do much more than take the edge off everywhere else.

"I lost my balance when you started to fall," I said.

Honestly, that sounded like a perfect analogy for our whole relationship. I lost my balance the moment we met. I started to tip forward slowly but now... I couldn't seem to stop the momentum. Every time I was around him, it became more difficult to imagine being anywhere else.

"Let me send a copy to Alice and see what she has to say," he suggested. "If she agrees it's a bad idea to post it online, then we won't."

I nodded slowly, my eyes on the dancing flames. "And if she thinks it's a good idea, then we will."

I felt better with the decision taken out of my hands. Maybe it was a cop out, but this way I didn't have to take responsibility for the fallout. Except in the back of my mind where I had to admit to myself I hadn't wanted to let go of Nate.

The kiss awakened something inside me. Something I buried for a very long time. The courage to live my life. To take chances. To let myself fall.

If we weren't pushed, I might have jumped in with him. Not with my shoes or hoodie on, but jumped, nonetheless. When he started to go, I held on tighter, letting him pull me with him. The icy cold water was a thrill I'd never experienced before.

Was this how Gran felt when she did adventurous things? The rush of adrenaline? The joy of being alive? Jumping into a cold creek on a winter day was probably nothing to her. Chances were, she did it regularly. But for me, letting go was intoxicating. I wanted more of it.

"That was awesome." Cadence stepped over beside me, her hands held up to the fire.

"I guess I should have dragged you in with me," I teased. "It's not too late to throw you in."

She made a face at me. "No way. It's cold enough out here."

I turned around so my back was to the fire. "You seem to be enjoying yourself here." I watched her sitting with Lucy and Tessa, giggling like a normal teenager over a social media reel, or something.

She shrugged. "It's okay. It's still bumfuck nowhere." And yet there was an edge to her voice. Like she also got a glimpse of life she could have had if she had siblings around her the way Lucy and Tessa did. Or, at least, a stable home life and friends.

She deserved all of that and so much more.

"Yeah, but it's a nice bumfuck nowhere," I said.

It wasn't until I noticed she and Nate were staring at me that I realized I actually said a curse word.

To be honest, that was almost as liberating as falling in the creek. After all, they were just words. No amount of f-bombs was going to bring my father back. It never would have. He made his decision long before I ever knew I had a sister. He was never going to stay with me and Mom. If it wasn't Cadence's mother, it would have been someone else.

Hell, maybe it was someone else as well. Who knew how many other siblings I might have out there that I didn't know about? *Cadence's siblings too*, I reminded myself.

If they all turned up, my doorstep was going to be a busy place. If they existed at all. They might not. I may never know.

"It's the best bumfuck nowhere," Nate said. "But

we should probably get dry and warm before we freeze. I prefer to skate on ice than turn into it."

"Will you be okay out here?" I asked Cadence. Nate was right. I needed to change into something dry and maybe have a hot cup of tea or coffee.

My clit reminded me of something else I could have that was hot. Maybe it was time I started taking some more chances.

"I'll be fine. I'm a big girl, remember?" She gave me a look like how could I possibly forget, before walking back over to Lucy and Tessa.

"Yeah, you are," I whispered.

"They grow up so fast," Nate said, grinning.

I socked him on the chest with the back of my hand. "At least you got to see your family grow up. I've missed everything with my sister." I exhaled out my nose. "I'm sorry. Come on, let's go and get warm."

I turned and slogged back to the house, my shoes squelching with every step, very aware of the tall, muscular hockey player who walked beside me.

"Just so you know, I didn't know the twins were going to push me," he said. "This wasn't some elaborate plot to get you naked."

"Sure it wasn't," I teased. "Are you sure you and

your sister didn't get together and hatch a devious plan?"

"They can't keep a secret, so no," he said. "They would have told you all about it, knowing them. Jamie too."

"Hmmm, I think I believe you." I felt bad for dripping on the hardwood floors all the way through the house and up the stairs, but if Chip and Hank hadn't shoved Nate, we'd be dry. At least, I would. With that in mind, I didn't feel so bad after all.

"I'll let you have the shower first," he said as we reached the bathroom. He pulled off his shirt and squeezed it out over the bathtub.

I swallowed. "Or we could...share?"

His eyes almost fell out of his face. His mouth dropped open like it was on a hinge. He stared at me for a moment before closing his mouth and letting it curve into a smile.

"I can share." He closed the door behind us and locked it. Eyes on mine, he stepped over to me and cupped my head with his hands. Like a man who hadn't eaten in days, he slammed his mouth down onto mine, slanting his face to kiss me deeply.

I kissed him back, my hands resting on his impossibly firm chest.

His hands dropped from my head, down to the

hem of my hoodie. He gripped it and pulled it and my drenched shirt up and over my head.

I raised my arms to help him with all the saturated fabric. He tossed everything into the bath and stood back to look at me, standing in wet jeans and a bra.

"You're so fucking gorgeous," he whispered.

My heart in my throat, I reached back to unhook my bra and shrug out of it. I tossed it onto the pile of clothes in the bath.

"Breathtaking," he whispered. He knelt in front of me to undo my jeans and pull them down my hips. When they reached my ankles, he raised one foot, then the other to tug off my shoes.

He stood and shimmied out of his track pants, revealing toned thighs, the V of his hips and his erection, which stood proud in his boxer briefs.

"And you call me breathtaking," I said appreciatively.

"That's because you are." He leaned over to turn on the water in the shower.

When the room was starting to fill with steam, I hooked my fingers in the waistband of my panties and pushed them down to my feet. I stepped out of them and into the shower.

I turned just in time to watch him push his

underwear off and step in behind me. My eyes were about to jump out of my head now. He was so big.

"Turn around." He picked up the soap and waited until I did what he said to start washing my back. "Good girl."

If he kept saying things like that, my clit was going to go absolutely wild. I forced a few breaths in and out, and let myself enjoy the heat of the water warming me up from the outside in. Or maybe it was his touch. He was firm but gentle at the same time. Confident and thorough.

"Face me," he said.

Without thinking, I straight away turned around.

"Good girl," he said again.

He started a careful wash of the front of me, starting with my throat and moving gradually down. Giving my breasts and nipples extra attention. He looked me in the eyes again before planting a gentle kiss onto each sensitive, hardened peak. The light, gentle touch sent a wave of need all the way through me. I didn't want to hold anything back from him, not tonight.

Tonight, I wanted to give him everything. My whole body.

Maybe my heart too.

The rest of my body was jealous of my nipples

and the attention he gave them, but he soon moved down over my belly before kneeling in front of me and washing my feet and working back up. Leaving my pussy for last.

After carefully washing me there, he put the soap aside, gently parted my thighs with his hands and pressed his face between them.

I closed my eyes, leaned against the tiled wall and let him taste me with his expert tongue. He seemed to know exactly what I liked and how I liked it. And he was more than generous in giving it to me. First with his mouth, then with his fingers as well. Pushing deep inside me and driving me all the way to the edge and over.

Right there against the shower wall, I shattered into a million pieces, so hard I couldn't keep from crying out his name. I wasn't sure if I even remembered mine, but I'd never forget his.

He worked me until I came back down to earth. Rising to his feet, he took my hands.

"I'm going to get you dry, and then I'm taking you to bed."

Chapter Twenty-Two

Nate

I wrapped my woman in a fluffy towel and dried her off carefully.

"I'll sort those out later." I nodded towards our damp clothes that lay scattered through the bath. Right then, I only had one thing on my mind. Making Oaklyn come again. Hearing her cry out my name the first time was most intoxicating. I was instantly addicted. I needed more and I needed it soon.

I unlocked the bathroom door and eased it open just a crack. "The coast is clear."

From the sound of laughter coming from outside, everyone was still around the fire, enjoying themselves and each other's company. They wouldn't see us sneak through the cottage dressed only in navy blue towels.

"Are you sure?" Oaklyn peered past my shoulder.

"We can make it two feet to our bedroom without being seen," I assured her.

"That's at least three feet," she said.

I looked over my shoulder at her and grinned. "It's two if we run."

"I don't think that's how distances work." She clutched the top of her towel to hold it over herself.

"They do now." I took her other hand and we dashed for our bedroom. The door was closed, so I had to twist the knob, push it open and drag her inside with me. Laughing, I closed the door and locked it again.

My back to the door I turned to face her. "See? Nothing to it."

She was laughing too. "I'm sure we made it by the skin of our teeth."

"The skin of somewhere, but maybe not our teeth." I pinched a section of my towel and pulled it free, letting the fabric drop to the floor.

Her gaze dipped to my cock, which was pointing at her, bobbing as I stepped closer to her. I grabbed a handful of her towel and pulled her closer to me.

"You're so fucking beautiful." I brushed my lips over hers.

"No, you are," she said before she kissed me back. Whatever reservations she had, she seemed to have put them aside for now. Instead, letting go and living in this moment.

I chuckled against her mouth. "I don't think anyone has called me beautiful before."

"Then they aren't looking properly." She placed a hand on my chest before trailing it slowly down over my abs and flat stomach. "You're a work of art. Are you sure you're real?"

"Cupcake, I'm a hundred percent real. I only look like this because I spend so much time in the staff gym, trying to impress you." Grinning, I flexed.

She batted my chest with the back of her hand. "Honeybun, you were this hot long before we met."

I cocked my head. "How do you know that? Oaklyn Walsh, have you been looking me up?" I hated to think what she saw and read about me.

"I might have," she said, tracing circles on my chest with the tip of her finger. Following the line of one tattoo, down to the next. Over to my shoulder and down my sleeve. "Do all of these mean something?"

"I thought they did." I looked down to where her

fingers rested on my bicep. "Then I met you. Now I know that they don't mean much. The only thing in my life that does is you."

"Nate..." she whispered.

I placed my finger under her chin and raised it so she was looking at me. "I mean it, Oaklyn. Before I met you, I was living, but now I feel alive. I never want anyone but you. The guy I was, that's not me anymore. I don't know if he ever really was. Everything felt empty, y'know?"

"I do know." She offered me a faint smile. "I've felt empty for a long time."

"I can fix that." I peeled open the front of her towel, revealing her glorious body, now warm and dry. When the fabric fell to the floor, I placed my hands on her shoulders and pushed her back until she was lying on the bed in front of me.

"You're the work of art," I told her.

I crawled up the bed to lie beside her and let my hands wander over her body, exploring every dip and curve of her skin. Every freckle, every scar.

"I'm falling for you, future Mrs. Southwell," I said.

She propped herself on her elbow, brow creased. "It's not real—"

I interrupted her. "It feels real. Everything about

this feels real. The way I feel about you, that's real. I know you feel the same way." I silently dared her to deny it.

Her lips moved, but she didn't contradict me.

"That's what I thought," I said. "Now, be a good girl and get on your hands and knees."

Her eyes went dark and she rolled over, quickly doing what I told her to. Displaying her perfectly rounded ass in front of my face.

I was going to come too soon if I wasn't careful. I forced myself to think of unsexy things. Zack. Skunks. A goat eating my cock.

I gripped her hips with my hands and kissed her ass before lightly biting down on the firm flesh.

She let out a squeak, but didn't pull away.

Smiling to myself, I ran my hands across her belly and over her firm, delicious breasts.

"I'm clean," I said. "I got everything tested shortly after I met you." For this exact moment. Because I knew I'd be making love to her and I wanted to be careful and ready.

She froze. Sagged slightly. She twisted around and sat on the bed. Her entire expression changed. Gone from wanting to embrace life, to what I can only describe as deeply sad.

"I'm clean too," she said quickly.

"That's good," I said carefully. I was missing something here and I couldn't figure out what it was. "You're on birth control?" If she wasn't, I had no problem using a condom. Whatever my woman wanted, I'd give it to her.

She shook her head slowly. "I'm not. I don't need to."

I shook my head. "I don't understand." She was trying to tell me something but I didn't know what.

She closed her eyes and looked pained. "I can't get pregnant. I don't have..."

She blew out a slow breath. "I have endometriosis. I had a hysterectomy because the pain was too much." She opened her eyes and looked at me, silently begging me to understand. Not to judge her.

"It took years to find a doctor who'd listen to me. They kept saying I'd want children some day. Or I'd get married and my husband would want children." Her tone was bitter now.

"Finally, I found one who understood. It's going to take a lifetime to pay it off, but the pain was... debilitating. So... I can't have a baby of my own."

"I see," I said slowly. I wanted to track down every doctor who hadn't paid attention to her needs and punch them in the face. Wasn't it their job to make sure their patients weren't suffering? What sort of stupid ass comment was it to suggest her future partner's opinion was more important than her body? They shouldn't be fucking practicing medicine, if you asked me.

"Do you?" she asked. "You said this feels real, but it can't be. It can't go any further than this. I can't give you what you need. I saw you with your nieces and nephews. You'll be an amazing father someday. Much better than mine. You need to find a woman who can give that to you." She sniffed softly.

I frowned at her. "You really think I'm going to walk away because you can't carry a child?"

This wasn't the conversation I expected to have with her tonight, but clearly this was important to her. And if it was important to her, then it was important to me.

She turned her face away from me.

I gripped her chin between my thumb and forefinger and turned her back to me.

"Oaklyn, I told you you're what I need. *You.* Would I like to be a father someday? Sure, but there's more than one way to do that. We're going to foster Cadence. Why should she be the only one? There's loads of kids out there who need a safe, loving home. We can give them that. If they aren't biologically ours, who cares? I don't. I don't need you to have my baby. You're perfect just as you are."

I leaned down to brush my lips over hers. "You're going to be an amazing mother some day, if that's what you want."

If it wasn't, that was okay too. We could always get a pet if she preferred that. I already planned to mentor young hockey players when I retired. Maybe coach a junior league. There were plenty of ways to be a carer without being a parent.

I thought back to the expression on her face when she watched Chip and Hank with Danny. And the way she was always so worried she wasn't enough for Cadence. I knew the answer to my question before she even spoke.

"It is what I want," she whispered. "I want to give my children a better life than I had. A better life than I *have*." She let her gaze wander over me. "Although, this is pretty good."

"Pretty good?" I raised an eyebrow at her. "Just pretty good?" I grabbed her wrists and pinned her arms above her head before straddling her hips.

"Okay, better than pretty good," she conceded. "Thank you. For understanding and not judging me."

"It's my pleasure." As if I would have judged her.

What she had to do, she never would have done lightly. I could only imagine the kind of pain she must have endured every month. I'd had my share of injuries, and having to sit out of training and playing was hard enough without having to sit out of life.

"Don't thank me yet, I'm not done with you," I added in a playful growl. "Now, I believe you're meant to be on your hands and knees?" I climbed off her and moved aside to give her room.

She slowly rolled back over and pushed herself onto all fours for me again.

I loved this side of her, letting me dominate her in the bedroom. She made me harder than ever. This woman was everything and then some.

"Good girl." I knelt behind her, my hands on her hips again. I wanted to hold back, but I couldn't. I notched my cock in her entrance before sliding myself all the way inside her.

"Fucking hell, you feel incredible," I whispered. I could have stayed like that forever, but my balls insisted I start moving, thrusting slowly in and out of her, while my hands roamed over her breasts, making her nipples hard. Down to her clit where I touched her until she moaned.

"Come with me," I insisted. I was so close to losing it, but I needed her there with me.

"I—" She moaned out my name before shattering around me, taking me with her.

The world disappeared, replaced with nothing but pleasure as I lost myself deep inside my woman. Finally claiming her. Making her mine.

I was in love with this woman.

I knew right then and there, I was going to make her my wife, for real.

Chapter Twenty-Three

Oaklyn

I woke warm and comfortable, safer than I ever remembered feeling. A little sore, but completely satisfied.

Nate hadn't let me rest until my body was Jell-O. He coaxed a third, then a fourth orgasm out of me when I didn't think I had any left to give. He'd persisted, insisting I could do it for him. Praising me every time I did.

I'd never been praised before. I liked it. More than liked it. Hearing it from his lips, it was hot as hell.

I opened my eyes a crack to see him looking back at me. His hair had grown out a little in the last handful of weeks. It was starting to curl around the back of his neck and the top of his head. I imagined he'd have a mop of curls if he let it grow out more.

"Morning, beautiful," he said, sounding sleepy still.

"Morning, honeybun," I teased. My heart flipped when he grinned in response.

"Sleep well, cupcake?" He brushed hair off the side of my face and ran his knuckles down my cheek.

"Better than I have in a long time." Judging by the faint light in the gap between the curtains, it was still early.

"Me too." He stretched, arms over his head before stifling a yawn with his fist. "Hungry?"

"Starving." My stomach was rumbling. We ate a huge dinner of roast beef and vegetables before the bonfire, but I'd worked off all of that overnight.

"Sounds like we're just in time to rustle up some breakfast." He cocked his head.

I listened too. Someone downstairs was rattling around pots and pans. That was followed by a squeal of laughter from one of the young twins.

The maternal yearning I always experienced was still there, but it was lessened now.

Nate was right. There were many other ways to become a parent. I had a lot of love to give to kids who badly needed it. For the first time, I have serious consideration about not moving on when my time at the arena finished.

Maybe I could put down roots in Lowball Bay after all.

"I just realized something," Nate said reluctantly.

I turned back to him, concerned. "What's that?"

"In order to go down there and eat, we'll have to get dressed," he said.

"That's usually how it works in a house full of people," I said.

Unless you were Gran, who may not care. If anyone was going to parade around naked, it would be her. Fortunately, I hadn't witnessed that. Yet.

"Yes, but I like you naked." Nate rolled over until he was lying over me and pinned me to the bed while he kissed me. His stomach rumbled loudly, drawing a giggle from me.

"It seems like your body has different priorities," I said.

He made an exaggerated face, but rolled off me. "That'll have to wait till later then. Besides, the twins will come looking for us if we're not up soon."

"We wouldn't want to traumatize anyone that young," I said. I pushed off the covers and climbed out of bed and over to my suitcase to pull out a change of clothes.

"We should definitely wait a few years before we traumatize them," Nate said with a laugh. He pulled on a pair of dark blue boxer briefs and tugged track pants over them. He might have a point about getting dressed being a shame. It was almost criminal to cover that chiselled body of his.

"You have something specific in mind?" I leaned against the wall to pull on a pair of leggings, and threw on an oversized hoodie over that.

"To traumatise them with?" he asked. "Not specific, no. That's more Blake Eastwood's department. He'd think of something different. Maybe a herd of sheep in their bedroom."

"I have a feeling they'd enjoy having sheep in their bedroom," I said.

Nate chuckled and pulled on a shirt over his tattooed arms and torso. "See? I'm not good at coming up with traumatic pranks."

"I'm sure you could if you tried," I told him. "I've heard the most traumatic ones involve glitter."

He stopped in the middle of pulling on a dry, clean hoodie. "Why does it sound like you practiced pranking people?" he asked, giving me a Cadence-worthy side eye.

"I have zero experience pranking people," I assured him. "But I read Pippa Grant books and her characters are experts."

He didn't look like he quite believed me, but he finished pulling on his hoodie and sat down to put on sneakers.

"Ready, cupcake?" He held his hand out to me.

I hesitated. Grimaced. "Everyone is going to know what we did, aren't they?"

He grinned slowly. "I'm going to say yes. Yes, they will. But we are engaged, remember? It's expected of us."

I didn't correct him by reminding him this was fake. He was right, it didn't feel fake anymore, but that was a conversation for later. Right now, I just wanted to have something to eat and check that Cadence was still okay.

I slipped my hand into his and we walked together down the stairs and into the large country cottage-style kitchen. Right down to the checked, gingham curtains, this place was an adorable, small farmhouse. And it smelled like cooking bacon.

"Smells like you killed a hog for me, sis." Nate stepped over to Jamie to kiss her cheek.

She swatted him away with her spatula and went back to turning the bacon in the heavy iron pan. "I sent Danny down to the store to buy a packet of bacon, but the eggs are fresh. And the girls made the bread." She nodded to a neatly sliced loaf that sat on a wooden cutting board, on the butcher block island.

"What do you grow here?" I asked.

She glanced around and grinned at me. "Apart from rowdy kids? We grow asparagus, much to the kids' disappointment."

"We want to grow jelly beans," Hank declared. He and Chip were occupied setting the big farmhouse table for breakfast.

"They were disappointed to learn that we could grow kidney beans, or lima beans, but not jelly beans," Danny said as he stepped in through the back door and wiped his feet on the mat. He carried an armful of firewood over to the wood stove in the centre of the living room. A fire was dancing merrily inside, keeping the whole space warm.

"Yeah, this is the wrong climate for jelly beans," Nate said, pretending to look serious. "You need hot weather and unicorns for those."

"Unicorns aren't real, Uncle Nate," Tessa said as she stepped out of the room she shared with her sister. Lucy and Cadence were right behind her.

Nate blinked at her. "What?" He shook his head. "Does not compute. Of course unicorns are real.

They can only be seen by people who believe in them. That's the only reason you haven't seen one."

"I believe in unicorns!" Chip said. "I want a black one."

"Only my nephew would want a black one." Nate ruffled his hair.

"If they were real, I'd have a black one," Lucy said. "Mine would breathe fire too."

"Mine would breathe ice," Tessa said.

They both glanced at Cadence, who shrugged. "I'd prefer a dragon."

"That would be awesome," Lucy breathed. "We could fly everywhere instead of walking."

"I want a dragon!" Hank said. "I want a dragon that poops out jelly beans!"

"Just look what you started," I said to Nate under my breath.

He grinned. "I regret nothing." The twitch of his eyebrows suggested he wasn't talking about this conversation.

I was still trying to get my head around last night. The things he told me as well as the things we did. And the fact we slept together and he wasn't running away. Yet.

Okay, it didn't seem as though he was going to either. Not until I screwed up somehow and drove him away. Right now, I wasn't sure what that would take. Maybe not as much as it would have before we fucked.

"I didn't think you did," I said, forcing my mind back to the present. "You enjoy being an uncle, don't you?"

"What's not to love?" He looked fondly at his nieces and nephews. "I get to come in here, be cool, talk about unicorns, then hand them back to their parents. Actually, that last bit is the most difficult part. Having to leave and head back to the city. Sometimes I wonder what it'll be like to move back here to Highball Creek."

"There's a cranberry farm for sale a couple of miles down the road," Danny said. "You could do your bit for Thanksgiving lunch."

Jamie barked a laugh. "Could you imagine Nate farming?"

Nate sniffed, pretending to be offended. "I could totally farm if I wanted to. I might even look into that before we head back."

I wasn't sure if he was serious. Or if I could imagine him farming either. On the other hand, there'd be worse things than living out here.

Highball Creek seemed like a close-knit community. People who looked out for each other and took care of each other. Who picked each other up when they were down. That would be very different to living in the city where people mostly mind their own business. If my neighbors were going through anything, I'd never know.

"Breakfast is ready," Jamie said, serving the bacon and scrambled eggs onto large plates and placing them in the centre of the table. Bread, butter and a jug of milk joined them, along with cups of tea or coffee for those who preferred a hot beverage with their breakfast.

I sat down between Nate and Danny, with Cadence opposite me. Every now and again, she'd give me a look like she was measuring me up. There was no way she was going to ask what went on last night, but she knew.

I met her gaze and gave her a smile before turning my attention to the delicious breakfast. What else could I do? Nate and I were both consenting adults and I didn't regret a moment of it. If anything, I looked forward to the next time he filled me with his thick, hard cock. Not only was he huge, but he knew exactly how to use it, as well as his hands and mouth. If I wasn't careful, he'd spoil me for everyone else.

In the back of my mind, I knew there would be

no one else, but I couldn't let that thought in too far. Not yet. This was too new, too fragile. And this place was magical. When we got back to the city, back to reality, everything might change.

That thought made my heart hurt more than I ever would have expected it to. In spite of myself, I was falling for my fake fiancé.

I was almost finished when I heard Nate's ringtone. It seemed to be coming from the kitchen. The sound was strangely muffled.

He pushed himself away from the table and walked towards the sound, looking this way and that. He opened a drawer just as the phone stopped.

"Is that where you went?" He pulled out the phone and glanced at the screen as it started to ring again. "Oaklyn, it's your grandmother." He handed me the phone.

"Excuse me." I pushed my chair back and stepped away from the table. I moved a polite distance before hitting the button to accept the call and putting the phone to my ear.

"Gran, is everything okay?" I asked.

Both Nate and Cadence watched me. Both with matching, worried expressions.

"I tried calling your phone, but I got no answer," she said.

"It had a swim," I said, glancing at Chip and Hank. They grinned back at me. I shook my head and turned my attention back to the phone call. "Is anything wrong?"

"I'm sorry to spoil your fun, but I think you should head home early," Gran said. "Your mother is here."

Chapter Twenty-Four

Nate

OAKLYN DIDN'T SAY MUCH ON THE DRIVE HOME. She sat and looked out the window, her lips pressed tight together.

Cadence was likewise silent. She was visibly annoyed when we dragged her away from her new friends so much earlier than planned. She'd stomped up to the room she shared with them and violently threw her belongings back into her backpack. She'd stomped back down, said her quiet goodbyes to Lucy and Tessa and stalked out to slide into the back of the SUV and slam the door behind her.

Oaklyn gave her a regretful look, but hadn't said anything. She clearly felt bad for dragging her away from a place where she was comfortable.

"We can come back any time," I'd said, but that

hadn't seemed to help very much, so I stayed silent too, instead humming along to Clint Stone, the country singer who had a house in Highball Creek.

He was off touring the world at the moment, otherwise he might have been at the fire the night before. I didn't know him well, but I liked his music. And since neither of the women in the car objected, I let it play. Honestly, I didn't think either of them heard it anyway. Cadence had her earbuds in and Oaklyn was lost in her own thoughts.

"Home sweet home," I said, hitting the button on the keychain to open the front gate and garage door. Another car was parked out front behind Gran's. I presumed it belonged to Caroline, Oaklyn's mother.

I'd barely turned off the engine and closed everything behind us when Cadence hopped out of the car and disappeared into the house.

"She's really upset," Oaklyn said, watching the way she'd gone. "Maybe we should have... I don't know."

"She'll be okay." I wrapped my arms around her and pulled her in for a hug. "And so will you. Are things between you and your mother that bad?"

"They've never been bad, not exactly," she said slowly. "After Dad left, they became strained. We found it harder to talk to each other. She's probably going to be pissed that I didn't tell her about Cadence. Gran must have."

I brushed hair off the side of her face and kissed her forehead. "She was going to find out soon or later."

"I was hoping for later," Oaklyn said. "Maybe when Cadence was about thirty. That would have given Mom a few extra years to get over the past."

"She might be here so she can get to know her," I suggested.

Oaklyn looked up at me, clearly disbelieving that possibility.

"Cadence is your sister," I said. "Give your mother the benefit of the doubt until you know the real reason why she's here. Okay? Innocent until proven guilty and all that."

"Yeah," she said softly. "I guess I shouldn't jump to conclusions." She didn't look convinced. "I guess we should go inside."

I would have preferred to press her up against the side of my black SUV and make love to her, but I guessed we should get this over with first.

I grabbed out our bags and followed her through the doorway that led from the garage into the house, kicking it shut behind me.

"Hi, Mom."

Gran and a woman who looked like a darker version of Oaklyn, were sitting in the living room, drinking coffee. Gran looked like she was at home here, but Caroline looked uncomfortable as hell.

"Oaks." Caroline rose to give her daughter a brief hug. In linen pants and a maroon mohair sweater, she couldn't have looked more different from her mother or her daughter.

In heels, she was taller than both of them. "Gran says you're engaged. And your sister turned up out of the blue. Why am I hearing about this from her and not from you?"

She looked accusingly at Oaklyn, then at me. She certainly had her mother's bluntness, if nothing else.

Oaklyn glanced at me. "We were going to tell you," she said. "We've been busy with getting Cadence settled in school and a bunch of other things."

Gran snorted softly, but went on sipping her drink.

Caroline looked equally sceptical. "I suppose I know now." She looked at me appraisingly. "You're the fiancé."

"Guilty." I gave her a grin and offered her my

hand which she glanced at but didn't shake. Before it became awkward, I lowered it to my side.

"You're a bit young, aren't you?" she asked.

"The heart wants what the heart wants," I said. "Oaklyn and I have been making it work." At least she wasn't accusing me of being a player. Yet. It had only been two or three minutes.

"And where is Prudence?" Caroline glanced around, although it was obvious the teenager wasn't in the room.

"Her name is Cadence, Mom," Oaklyn said patiently. "She should be in her room. She'll come down when she gets settled in again."

"There's a delivery for you," Gran said, waving to the coffee table.

Visibly glad for the distraction, Oaklyn picked up the small box. "It's addressed to me." Her gaze slid to me.

What could I do but grin back? "Open it."

She shook her head slightly, but tore open the box. "It's a new phone. When did you do this?" She frowned at me.

"This morning, before breakfast," I said simply. "I figured since yours was trashed when we fell in the creek, you'd need a new one." Given it was my nephews who pushed us in, it was the least I could do. Besides, I wanted to buy it for her.

"This must have cost a fortune," she said.

Caroline was looking at me with a creased brow. "You bought her a phone?"

"Isn't that something fiancés are supposed to do?" I asked. "Make sure their women have everything they need."

"In my experience, men often like to buy gifts when they're feeling guilty," Caroline said flatly.

"The only thing I'm guilty of is being in love with your daughter," I said. "It was my nephews who trashed her phone. She was going to need a new one anyway, so why not organize one for her?"

Caroline looked at me like I was full of shit. Like somehow I was trying to compensate for something. Evidently what her former husband did to her still stung.

"Oaklyn told me what her dad did," I said slowly.

Caroline winced. "She shouldn't have..."

"I didn't have much choice with Cadence turning up," Oaklyn said. "But I don't want to keep any secrets from him." She pulled the phone out of the box and turned it on.

"Thank you." She kissed my mouth. Her touch

was soft, but it sent a jolt of electricity all the way through my body.

Think unsexy thoughts, I told myself once again. It was difficult around her. All I wanted to do was give her orgasms. Lots of them.

"Anything for my cupcake," I told her. I put an arm around her and held her close to me, my body pressed to hers.

"Will you be staying with us?" I asked Caroline. "I have a very nice spare room with your name on it. You'll have your own bathroom too." It didn't hurt to try to butter up my future mother-in-law. Right?

In time, she'd come to see that I wasn't like her former husband. Not even a little bit.

"Just for a couple of nights," Caroline said. "Then I have to get back. Robert will worry if I'm gone too long." Her expression softened, making her look more like Oaklyn.

They were both hard as nails on the outside, but with a softer interior. Kinda like me.

"Great," I said with more enthusiasm than I felt. Oaklyn didn't look too happy to learn her mother would be sticking around for longer. But she wouldn't have sent her away either, so it seemed we were stuck with her for now. Honestly, since that would give me more time to win her over,

I decided it wasn't a bad thing. I'd turn on the charm until she liked me as much as her own mother did.

"Don't want Robert to worry," Gran said.

I couldn't tell what her opinion of Caroline's husband was, but she must have preferred him to her first husband. He sounded like a vast improvement on a man who'd cheat and have a family with another woman. I still couldn't get my head around that.

"Gran," Oaklyn said wearily. "Can you not provoke each other?"

Gran raised a hand in the air. "Who's provoking anyone? I was agreeing with her. Robert is a worrier. He'd be here too if he wasn't scared of flying."

"He's not scared of flying," Caroline argued. "He just...doesn't like it. And anyway, he couldn't get time off work. He's a lawyer," she said to me. Then to Oaklyn, "A divorce lawyer, if you ever need one."

"Mom." Oaklyn sighed. "We're not even married yet."

"Yet," I agreed. "But that's just a formality. Right, cupcake?" I raised my eyebrows at her.

"Right, honeybun," she said. "Just a formality."

"Have you set a date?" Gran asked.

"We were thinking summer," I said before

Oaklyn could answer. "In the off-season. Maybe we could have a wedding on the beach."

"Off-season from what?" Caroline asked. Apparently Gran hadn't told her everything.

"Nate is a professional ice hockey player," Oaklyn said. "He's a defenseman for the Lowball Bay Sea Dragons." She seemed torn between pride, and worry about what her mother might think.

"You're a hockey player?" Caroline narrowed her eyes at me.

I responded with the biggest grin I could manage. "Guilty as charged, ma'am."

"That means you travel a lot," she said.

"Yes, I do. That's why we asked Gran to move in here too," I said evenly. "So Oaklyn has people around her when I'm not here. The last thing I want is for her to be alone and feeling neglected. That's also why she needs a phone. So I can call her every night while I'm away."

"I've heard what men like you get up to when they travel a lot," she said dryly.

"That's why she married Robert," Gran said. "He hates to travel."

Caroline shot her a look over her shoulder. "That's not the only reason I married him."

Gran cackled. "You're not denying it's part of it."

Caroline turned away from her. She looked as though she was about to set me straight.

Before she could, I said, "I'm devoted to Oaklyn. Ever since I met her, I haven't been able to look at another woman. I don't want to now and I never will. She's my everything. I get you went through awful stuff, but I am never going to do that to her. I can promise all of you that. I'd rather cut off my left ball than hurt her."

"If you hurt Oaklyn, I think Caroline will want the right one too," Gran said.

"She can have it," I said without reservation. "If I do anything to break her heart, I don't deserve either of them."

Without her, they'd turn blue and fall off anyway. I might as well give them away.

"I—" Oaklyn started to speak when the doorbell rang.

"That would be the other surprise I have for you," I said. "I know you said you could buy your own flowers, but I couldn't resist." I stepped over to open the door and take the delivery from the driver's hand. I gave him a generous tip and closed the door before turning back to Oaklyn, a bouquet of a dozen red roses in my hand.

She was white as a sheet, staring at the flowers.

Chapter Twenty-Five

Oaklyn

Sixteen years earlier

I lay on my bed until I heard voices downstairs. No shouting, no anger. Just the regular, day-to-day voices of my parents.

Did my mother know my father had another family? How could she know and still look him in the eyes? I didn't want to see his face, much less have a conversation with him. I felt like he'd ripped my heart in a million pieces and threw them into Puget Sound.

I eased the covers off myself and stepped over to the door.

Dad knocked on it and asked to come in and talk

to me, but I'd ignored him. What was I supposed to say? I had no words to describe how betrayed I felt. How absolutely floored. Assuming the kid was biologically his, then I had a sister.

Maybe she wasn't his, but I knew in my heart she was. Did the other woman know about my mother and me? She seemed to. And yet, she hadn't sent him away. She had a baby with a man who had a family. A man who didn't care about us enough to be faithful. It wasn't just cheating, he had a whole other life.

I was starting to think I didn't know him at all. Who was this man I called father? He felt like a total stranger.

I unlocked the door as quietly as I could and eased it open.

Just at that moment, my mother laughed at something my father said. Everything down there sounded normal, when this day was anything but.

I moved slowly and silently to the top of the stairs and down. I didn't want to look at him, but I had to. I had to see the expression on his face when he saw me. I had to understand what was going on, why he'd do this. I had to know if my mother already knew. If she did, then everything I thought I knew about my life was a lie.

If she knew he had another family, then she was lying to me as well.

I reached the bottom of the stairs and headed into the kitchen. My mother was busy placing a bouquet of fresh flowers into a vase.

Not just any flowers, but roses. Her favorite. He only bought those on special occasions. Her birthday, Mother's Day, Valentine's Day. And apparently when he was caught fucking around with another woman.

Dad stood at the sink, washing a colander full of cherries. Not just any cherries, but my favorite. Rainier cherries.

Yeah, he knew he fucked up all right.

He glanced over at me, guilt etched on his features.

"There you are," he said, trying to speak in his usual tone, but more careful, as if he was worried I'd blurt out the truth. "I thought I'd stop for some of these on the way home." He held up the colander, water dripping from the holes underneath.

"Yeah, cool." I stepped over to the fridge, opened it and pulled out the milk. I poured myself a glass. "Nice flowers."

"They're beautiful," Mom gushed. "They must have cost a fortune." She looked a sidelong at Dad.

"You're worth it," he told her.

If he could afford another family, he could afford to buy my mother roses. All the roses she could handle. I wanted to pull out the thorns and scratch him with them.

"Oh, you." She finished fussing over the flowers. "I'll be back in a moment to start dinner." She kissed his cheek and headed out of the room.

"Oaklyn," Dad started. He paused and pressed his lips together. "Why were you coming home from school so early?"

Because that was the issue here. I gave him my best glare. "Period pain."

He frowned, his expression almost worried. Okay, he did look worried, but I didn't need it from him. "Should you see a doctor? You've missed so much school because of it."

Now he cared?

"I'm fine." I gulped down my milk and placed the glass down on the countertop a bit too hard.

"What you saw—"

I cut him off with a glance. "Mom doesn't know."

He looked down towards the floor.

Yeah, that was what I thought.

"Are you going to tell her?" I asked.

"Tell me what?" Mom asked, stepping back into the kitchen.

Dad spoke before I could. "Oaklyn came home early because of bad period pain. I think she should see a doctor."

Now my mother looked worried, but her worry was all about me, not about being caught screwing up. "Again? I think that's a good idea. I'll book you in as soon as I can get an appointment." She put her arm around me and gave me a squeeze before opening the fridge and pulling out some meat for dinner.

"Do you feel up to eating?" she asked me.

I wanted to say, 'Not with him,' but she seemed so happy. I couldn't bring myself to tear her world in half. Not yet. She'd be devastated. She'd feel the same way I did. Like everything she thought she knew was a lie. Like the ground under her feet was rippling with an earthquake. She wouldn't trust him again. Neither would I.

If a man I thought cared about me could do this, then what else could he do? He might have a dozen other families out there in the city. Tons of other children. Other lives.

Looking at him felt like I was looking at a complete stranger. One I'd never believe again. As far as I was concerned, I only had one parent. One person I could trust. One person who wouldn't betray me how he had.

I promised myself I would never put myself in her position. I'd never let anyone do to me what he'd done to her.

I swear I could see the roses wilting as they sat in the vase, dying moment by moment because he'd bought them out of guilt. Maybe to soften the blow when he confessed what he did.

As if flowers would help.

Nothing would help. Nothing but never seeing him again.

Present day

"Oaklyn?" Nate's voice snapped me out of the past and back to the present. "If you don't like red, I can send them back for a different color."

"It's not the colour." Which I couldn't stop staring at.

They were the same shade my father used to buy for my mother. That perfect red, with the scent that tickled my senses. Somewhere between enjoyment and revulsion. Not because the scent wasn't beautiful, but because of the memories that crashed back into my mind. The feelings, raw like they'd happened yesterday.

"You don't like them, do you?" His face fell. "That's okay, I'll get rid of them."

"No," I said without thinking. "Don't do that." I took them from his hand and brought them to my chest. Inhaled the smell.

"They're beautiful. It was very thoughtful of you." But all I could do was wonder what he'd done. Were the flowers and phone bought out of guilt? Did he regret that we'd fuck— Slept together?

Tears stung my eyes but I blinked them away. Of course he did. He got what he wanted and now he was trying to figure out a way out. The easiest thing would be to pack up everything, including Cadence and leave.

I caught Mom staring at me.

No, not at me, at the roses. She clearly came to the same conclusion I had. What other reason does a man have for giving me these exact flowers?

"Oaklyn?" Nate asked tentatively. "Please talk to me."

"Those were the flowers her father used to give

to me because he felt guilty for fucking other women," Caroline said bluntly. "He thought they'd make everything okay. Somehow what he did, didn't matter if he brought me roses and other things. Asshole."

I couldn't remember having heard her swear before. The fact she did it now spoke volumes about how upset she was. Those roses must have taken her back to the past too.

He brought her roses before he told her he was leaving her for Rebecca. As if somehow that would soften the blow.

"Oh, shit," Nate whispered. "I had no idea, I swear. When you said you didn't need flowers, I thought you meant because you could buy them yourself. Not that they brought back bad memories. I'm such an idiot." He clapped a hand to his forehead.

I blinked away tears and lowered the roses. Looked over at him standing there with the heel of his hand pressed to the skin right above his left eye.

In that moment, I knew. He hadn't bought the flowers because he did anything wrong. He brought them because he loved me. Because he thought I needed something to brighten my day. Something to make it easier to deal with my mother turning up, and because Cadence had turned my life upside down.

He wasn't being guilty or sneaky, he was being sweet.

"You love me?" I whispered.

He gave me a lopsided, soft smile. "Yeah, I love you. From the first moment I saw you. The more I get to know you, the deeper I fall. You're the most amazing woman I've ever met. Well, you and Gran." He grinned.

"Damn right," Gran said.

Nate laughed and leaned over to offer her a fist bump before turning back to me. "I promise never to buy you flowers again. Unless you ask me to."

"No flowers," I said. "Except the ones in the garden. I don't mind if you want more of those out there, but not inside the house." They'd last longer out there anyway.

I swallowed back a knot of emotion. "I love you too."

I don't know when I'd fallen for him. Maybe it was when I fell with him into that frigid water. Chip and Hank did us a favor. They made me see what was right in front of me. What I wouldn't let myself see. This sweet, smart, funny man who adored me. Who I adored.

His life had also been turned upside down, but he'd rolled with it so he could be by my side through everything. While I tried to figure things out, he hadn't wavered. Not for a moment.

He took the roses from my hand and tossed them aside before wrapping his arms around me and kissing me, firmer and deeper than he'd kissed me before.

I wound my arms around his neck and kissed him with everything I had. I wanted him to know I had no doubts about us. For the last sixteen years, I'd searched for some stability, somewhere to belong.

After what my father did to my mother, I'd thought of men as the ones who created the turmoil. But it wasn't. Not for me. Moving from place to place and never even *trying* to settle down, that was why I never felt at home anywhere. I hadn't let myself stop and breathe. I hadn't let myself get close to anyone. Until now.

This man, he was not like my father. He couldn't be more different.

Nate was stability. He was love. He was home. *My* home. My heart. He was everything.

"I love you so much," I said into his ear.

I hesitated, not wanting to ruin the moment.

"There's something I should tell you." He

deserved to know Lacey would want her job back in a couple of months. I'd find something else in Lowball Bay, but I wouldn't be working at the arena anymore. He'd have to go back to working out in the player's gym instead. That was probably better for both of us anyway. I might take on some private clients. Either way, I wasn't leaving town.

Nate started to say something, but was interrupted by another ring of the doorbell.

I raised my eyebrows at him.

"I didn't buy anything else, promise." He peered through the window beside the front door. "It's Kymmie from social services. She must be here to assess our suitability to foster Cadence."

Chapter Twenty-Six

Nate

Oaklyn's eyes widened and she paled again.

Before she could freak out, I cupped her face with my hands and brought my nose down to hers. "We can do this. She just wants to look around to make sure things are safe here. That we don't have a herd of elephants stomping through the kitchen, or alligators in the bathtubs."

"No such luck." Gran sighed heavily. "Not even a swan in the pool."

"We get ducks sometimes," I told her.

"That's not even close to the same thing," she argued. She shook her head at me but smiled.

"I'll get you some swan earrings," I promised.

"Hot diggity." She did a happy dance in her seat.

Caroline made a face at her, like she was out of her mind.

"I'll get the door," I said. "Gran can you go and get Cadence from her room, please?"

"I will if Caroline promises not to say anything negative about her, or to her," Gran said. She looked down her nose at her daughter.

Caroline threw her hands up in the air. "I wasn't going to say anything."

"Gran is right," Oaklyn said. "Both of you be on your best behaviour. This is too important for us to fuck up now."

So important she was willing to swear to make her point. She was so stinking adorable.

I kissed her nose. "We've got this."

The doorbell rang again.

Oaklyn gripped my arm. "What if we say the wrong thing? What if she doesn't think we're suitable for Cadence?"

"We are," I said firmly. "She's not going to hold it against us if we say something dumb. And by we, I mean me. You'll do perfect. Come on, let's open the door."

She drew in a long, deep breath and let it out again through her nose. "Okay, we can do this." She nodded to me to open the door.

I unlocked it and pulled it open, smiling at Kymmie as though we hadn't all been losing our minds for the last couple of minutes.

"Hey, welcome to our home." I gestured around the room behind me with a flourish. "Please, come in."

Kymmie leaned against the door frame to pull off her shoes, then stepped inside.

Everything about her was completely professional. She wasn't going to be won over by a big house, professionally decorated and expensive. Of course not. That was just window dressing. Pretty window dressing, but still superficial.

"Oaklyn," Kymmie greeted her with a nod. "How have things been with your sister?"

"Good," Oaklyn squeaked. She cleared her throat. "Good," she said again, more clearly this time. "She's settling in nicely. Going to school and making friends. All the usual teenagery stuff."

My usual teenagery stuff consisted of driving around Highball Creek in an old, rusted out car, drinking too much bad vodka, and swimming in the creek. I was lucky I didn't drown or crash into more than a half dead tree that one time. Compared to that, Cadence's life was pretty solid.

Kymmie made a note on her tablet. "And you are?" she asked Caroline.

"My future mother-in-law," I said. "She's come to meet Cadence and celebrate our engagement. She's ecstatic for all of us."

"Thrilled to bits," Caroline said, sounding not thrilled to bits. She managed to force a smile that made her look constipated.

"Will you be living here too?" Kymmie asked.

"She's only staying for a couple of days," Oaklyn said.

"I see." Kymmie made another note on her tablet. "You won't mind me taking a look around?"

"Not at all," I said. "We'll give you the guided tour. Can I offer you a cup of coffee?"

Oaklyn looked at me like I was the one who lost my mind.

I gave her a questioning look back. Was there a problem with being hospitable?

"I'd love a cup," Kymmie said.

"Oaklyn and I will go and make it." I grabbed her wrist and pulled her towards the kitchen.

"Are you trying to bribe her?" Oaklyn whispered. She looked around my arm and smiled at Kymmie like nothing was wrong.

"I'm trying to be nice," I whispered back. "I only

offered coffee, not a Ferrari. Although, if she wants a Ferrari—"

"Nate! We're not bribing her with a Ferrari!" Oaklyn smiled at Kymmie again and gave her a little wave. "Just trying to figure out what kind of coffee to make. What would you prefer?"

"I'm used to terrible instant, so anything will be fine," Kymmie said.

"Now she thinks we're out of our minds," Oaklyn whispered.

"She doesn't think that," I assured her. "Why don't I make the coffee while you show her around?"

"Good, yes, good." Oaklyn nodded. "Let's do that." She stepped away and said, "Um, so this is the kitchen." She waved around at the space.

"It's very nice," Kymmie said. "Do either of you cook?"

"Is that a requirement for fostering?" Oaklyn frowned. "I mean, yes I can cook."

"I can cook," I said. "Sometimes it's even edible."

Oaklyn gave me another look, like I was digging us a bigger hole. "What Nate means is..." She stood with her mouth open, not coming up with an explanation for what I meant.

"Being able to cook isn't a requirement," Kymmie said. "Just a useful life skill." She looked at me like maybe I could stand to learn a thing or two.

"Oaklyn and Gran are teaching me how to cook better," I said. "And they're teaching Cadence too." That would have been news to everyone, including Cadence, but it seemed like the right thing to say.

Judging by the way Kymmie nodded approvingly, and made another note on her tablet, it was.

One point to Nate Southwell.

"Yes," Oaklyn said, seizing on the line of conversation. "She's very enthusiastic about learning."

"What's her favorite thing to cook?" Kymmie asked.

Oaklyn froze like a deer in headlights. "Um..."

"Clam chowder," I said. "The kid is practically obsessed with the stuff. Me too, if we're being honest here." At least some of that was true. She did enjoy her chowder, and so did I. As for making it, that was a whole other kettle of fish.

"What's not to love?" Kymmie asked. She accepted the cup of coffee I handed her with a grateful nod and took a sip. "This is very good coffee, Mr. Southwell."

"Please, call me Nate. I like a cup of good coffee." The stuff we got at the arena was pretty awful at the best of times, so when I was at home I splurged on better beans. As far as I was concerned, life was too short to drink bad coffee.

"I'll show you around the rest of the house," Oaklyn said. "Over there is the dining room, and there's another living area back there."

I leaned against the kitchen counter and let her show Kymmie around our home while sipping my own coffee.

"Does she really want this?" Caroline asked, keeping her voice down. "Fostering her sister. It's a lot of responsibility for someone she hardly knows."

"She wants this very much." I met her gaze unflinchingly. "I know it must have been hard on you, raising her by yourself."

"I tried to give her everything she needed." Caroline leaned on the countertop opposite me, her hands behind her. "When her father left, I... I unravelled. I thought we had everything. The perfect family. The perfect marriage. And then everything fell apart and I realized nothing about it was perfect. It never had been and I just hadn't wanted to see it. I knew something was up when he said he was working late. The trips he took out of town."

She shook her head. "All of the signs were there

and I didn't want to see them. And because I didn't, she was hurt. I don't want that to happen to her again."

"I would never do that," I assured her. "Oaklyn and Cadence are my family now. I guess that makes you and Gran my family too. She already said if I did anything wrong she'd cut off my dick and feed it to a goat."

Caroline snorted a laugh. "That sounds like my mother. I'm sure she threatened Robert with something like that too. Just between you and I, I think he's terrified of her." After a moment she added, "Robert is scared of a lot of things, but he's very sweet."

"He's a lucky guy," I said. "I can tell you love him a lot. And your daughter too. If you give her a chance, I know you'll love Cadence as well. She's a great kid. Smart as hell. She just needs solid ground under her feet. That's what we all want to give her. I hope you can be a part of that."

"No wonder my daughter loves you," Caroline said. "I think I might have underestimated you."

"It happens," I said lightly. "But I'm very wise for my age." I rubbed my chin as though stroking a long beard.

"That might be pushing it," she said dryly. "But I

think you might be good for my daughter. And if Cadence is going to be in both of your lives, then I better get to know her."

"She is," I said. "All of this is just a formality." I nodded in the direction Oaklyn had taken Kymmie.

"Does this make Cadence my granddaughter?"

The expression on her face was so much like Gran, I had to hold back a laugh. I wasn't sure whether she was joking or not.

"I don't think Cadence is going to be calling us Mom and Dad, so I think we can just keep with first names and know that sometimes family is more than blood."

"That's true," Caroline said softly.

"You have a lovely house," Kymmie was saying as she and Oaklyn reappeared. "It feels very homey. A nice place to have kids."

"It is," Oaklyn agreed. She looked slightly more relaxed than she had when Kymmie arrived. "It's big enough for lots of them. Nate and I are thinking about fostering more if this works out. We have lots of love to give."

"That's very commendable," Kymmie said. "The world needs more people like you. There are plenty of kids out there who need a stable home like this."

"We're more than happy to provide it," Oaklyn said.

Gran appeared in the doorway behind them. She mouthed something at me, but I couldn't make out what. I frowned at her and shook my head.

"I'll need to speak to Cadence now," Kymmie said. "Ultimately, it's up to her to decide if she's comfortable staying here. If that's the case, then I see no reason why we can't finalize her paperwork to make the fostering formal."

"That would be wonderful," Oaklyn said.

Gran raised her arms over her head and waved them back and forth at me. She mouthed something again, but I still couldn't figure out what she was trying to say. She dropped her arms quickly when Kymmie turned to look at her, a smile snapping onto her lips.

"Of course," Oaklyn said. "I know she'll be honest with you about her feelings. She's been very forthcoming since she arrived here."

"Great, can I see her then?" Kymmie asked.

Gran's eyes widened and she waved at me to come over to her.

"Excuse us for a minute." I stepped sideways past Oaklyn and over to Gran, who grabbed my arm and pulled me a couple of feet away. "What's going on?"

"Cadence is gone, is what's going on," Gran said. "Looks like she's packed up everything in her room and left."

Chapter Twenty-Seven

Oaklyn

I couldn't hear what Gran said, but judging by the expression on Nate's face it wasn't good. My heart sank. Of course this would all go wrong somehow.

Nate smacked a hand to his forehead. "I'm so sorry, we forgot Cadence went to hang out with a friend of hers." He flashed me a brief, reassuring smile that did nothing to reassure me. What the hell was going on?

"She's not here?" Kymmie asked.

I wanted the answer to that question too. As far as I knew, Cadence should be in her room, if she wasn't, then where was she?

"Like we said, she's making friends," Nate said quickly. "Oaklyn, cupcake, maybe you can give her a call and see what time she's headed home?" His eyes were wide and full of meaning. Meaning that came together very quickly in my head.

She wasn't here and she hadn't gone to hang out with any of her friends. I didn't know if she had any in the area. If that was the case, my worst fear had come to fruition.

Cadence had run away.

"Of course I can call her, honeybun," I said, trying to contain my panic. "I'll let her know Kymmie is waiting here to speak to her. I'm sure she won't want to miss you." Or she ran because she *knew* Kymmie was here.

"Please," Kymmie said. "I have another appointment I'll have to leave for shortly."

"I'm so sorry for the inconvenience," I said as sincerely as I could. I could only imagine how this must look to her. Cadence was supposed to make one of the biggest decisions of her life and she wasn't here for it. If we couldn't find her, there was only one way this was going to go. Kymmie would have no choice but to place her somewhere else.

Was that what Cadence wanted? She might have run away because she didn't want to be with us.

My heart tore into a thousand pieces.

"I'll call her." I pulled out my new phone and

tried to remember Cadence's number. After staring at the handset for a solid minute or two, I shook my head. "I'm sorry, this is a new phone. Her number isn't programmed into it."

"Try mine," Nate said. "It's..." He scrunched up his brow in thought. "Can I borrow your phone, cupcake?"

"Sure, honeybun," I said absently. I handed it to him and tried not to sigh. Where was his phone this time?

He pressed on the screen and tilted his head back, listening. After a moment, his ring tone sounded from the fruit bowl in the middle of the kitchen island. His phone stood, jutting out between two bananas.

"Huh, no idea how it got there." He quickly scrolled through his phone before putting Cadence's number in my contacts.

I stepped a few feet away and pressed on the number before putting the phone to my ear. After a few rings, it finally clicked.

"Hey, leave a message, or whatever." The phone beeped, went silent for a few heartbeats and then the call disconnected.

"It went to voicemail," I said. "She must not have heard it ring. I can try again."

"I really have to leave," Kymmie said apologetically. "I'll be in contact to make another appointment."

"I'm so sorry," I said again. "We didn't mean to be an inconvenience."

Why had Cadence chosen now to run? Did she feel like she couldn't talk to me about what she was thinking? Obviously she did, or would have stuck around to tell me what was on her mind.

I'd failed her and I didn't know if there was anything I could do to fix it.

"It happens," Kymmie said. "It's good to see she's spending time with friends."

I got the impression she didn't buy the story of my sister's whereabouts. Apparently I wasn't a good actor. Maybe I was so transparent Cadence saw through all my misgivings.

After the conversations she'd overheard, and then spending time with Nate's family, she must have felt like she didn't belong here. If that was the case, then where the hell had she gone?

"I'll see you out," Nate said. He led Kymmie over to the door and closed it behind her. Only when he was sure she'd gone, he turned to me. "We need to find her." His brow was creased with worry.

I shook my head slowly, my heart heavy. "I have no idea where to start."

"She can't have gone far," Caroline reasoned. "You only arrived back an hour and a half ago."

"She could have gone a long way on a skateboard," Gran said helpfully.

I gave her a dry look. "Unless you let her borrow your skateboard, then she's probably on foot."

"Then we search the neighborhood," Nate said. "Someone should stay here in case she turns up here."

"I'll stay," Caroline said.

Nate nodded. "The rest of us will split up and search. Stay in touch by phone."

"Make sure you *have* your phone," I said. His was in his hand a couple of minutes ago, and now it was beside the fruit bowl, like the bananas were a magnet.

He smiled, abashed, snatched it up and pushed it into his pocket. "One day I'll stop losing this thing."

I followed him and Gran to the front door. "Where do we even start?"

"We start walking and keep our eyes peeled," Gran said. She snagged her rainbow colored bucket hat from the hall table beside the door and jammed it onto her head. "She's probably sitting under a tree, on her phone half, a block away. Immersed in one of those video apps.”

“Or she took a bus and could be anywhere by now,” I said.

“Hey.” Nate put an arm around me. “We’ll find her, okay? We’ll find her and we’ll bring her home. Whatever’s going through her head, we’ll sort it out. You know why? Because that’s what families do. We take care of each other. Also, I’m going to send a message to the team group chat.”

He pulled his phone back out, quickly tapped on the screen, nodded in satisfaction and then pushed it back into his pocket.

“There’s a whole hockey team searching Lowball Bay for her. We’ll find her.”

I leaned against him. “I love you,” I whispered.

The way he cared about my sister, like he’d known her for years— I fell for him even harder. He’d never hesitated to be there for both of us. There was nothing he wouldn’t do for me or for her. Nothing I could ask that would be too much. He was a good man, the best.

“I love you too.” He kissed the top of my head. “Now, let’s go and find us a teenage runaway.”

“Let’s do it,” I said with a nod.

“After we find her,” he said with a wink.

I socked his chest with the back of my hand, but I was smiling. I couldn't wait to get naked with him again, but he was right, we needed to find Cadence first.

We stepped out into the cool afternoon. The temperature was dropping fast. We needed to find her before it got too cold. The idea of her shivering under a bridge somewhere...

Until right then, I hadn't fully appreciated how much she meant to me. I'd spent the last few weeks dithering and making excuses to myself. Making plans to leave town. Never letting myself get too comfortable. Never letting *her* get too comfortable.

When we found her, I was going to start making up for all of that. I had a lot of work in front of me, but I'd make the home for her that she deserved. The home neither of us ever had. Stable, permanent and loving.

"I'll go downhill," Gran declared.

"You don't have a skateboard hidden behind a tree, do you?" I asked.

She looked at me, grinned and headed off down the road with a swing in her step.

"Why am I thinking we should worry about her as much as we do Cadence?" I said with a groan.

"For two people not related by blood, they're a lot alike," Nate said. "Smart, sassy and adventurous."

"The opposite of me," I said.

"You're smart and sassy," he said. "And adventurous in all the ways that count." He squeezed my shoulders and stepped away. "I'll look uphill if you want to search down Ballsac Street?" He pointed towards the street that ran off this one.

"It's as good a place as any," I said. I kissed his mouth before I trotted away, scanning the street and the lawns in front of the houses, for my sister.

In this part of Lowball Bay, all of the homes were huge, the front of each neat and well maintained. There was nowhere for anyone to hide. If she was here, she'd be in plain sight. In theory.

She could have climbed a wall or hidden behind one of the wide oaks. Okay, that sounded like something out of a cartoon, but I had to bear every possibility in mind right now.

"Hey, we heard you need some help." Andi Welling was stepping out the front of her house, her partner Cam in tow, their hands joined. They both looked comfortable and casual in jeans and warm sweaters, the left winger towering over the team's owner.

"Yes I do, thank you." Gratitude swelled in my chest. "I thought you'd be at work."

Andi glanced back at Cam and smiled. "Cam had the afternoon off so we thought we'd...spend some time enjoying our new house."

Cam grinned.

"Oh." My face heated. That would explain why her red hair looked even messier than usual. "I'm sorry to interrupt."

"We were taking a snack break," Cam said. "We figured this was important, so here we are." He ran a hand over his head to smooth down his own hair.

"I appreciate it," I said. "If you can look around here, I'll keep going down the street."

When they nodded, I hurried on. Every now and again, pulling out my phone to see if my sister would answer. Each time, it went to voicemail. Each time, I left a message, becoming more and more frantic as she didn't respond.

"Cadence, please call me back," I begged. "I know things haven't been easy, but... We're family... and I love you." Unable to think of anything to say, I ended the call and sent the same message via text. Like the last five, it remained unread.

I started to think about all the things that might have happened to her. What if she got hit by a car, or kidnapped? What if she got on a bus and it crashed? What if an alien spacecraft appeared, beamed her up and flew away?

Okay, the last one was unlikely, but I wasn't ruling anything out right now. Including a herd of hungry goats. All I knew was she had to be somewhere and she had to be alive. I had too much to say to her. Too much to make up for. If she didn't want to live with us, I'd understand. I just wanted her to know how I felt. I wanted to be in her life, one way or another.

If she'd let me.

I reached the end of the street and stood looking up and down the main highway in and out of Lowball Bay. The bus stop was half a mile away, on the other side of the road.

It was empty. No teenager with her backpack waiting to board. If she went that way, she was gone already.

"Where are you?" I whispered.

The idea I may never see her again was becoming more and more difficult to ignore. She might leave and never come back, but she might also disappear without a trace. It was too soon to get the police involved, but I was ready to call nine one one any moment now. Would they listen if I begged them to help us look for her?

I all but jumped out of my skin when my phone rang. I pulled it out and put it to my ear without looking to see who it was.

"Cadence?" My heart was racing so hard I thought it might bounce out of my chest and across the highway. Traffic was moving so steadily, the chance of it reaching the other side without getting run over was ridiculously small.

"No, it's Gran. I have an idea of where she might be. I figured it was worth taking a look."

Chapter Twenty-Eight

Nate

I BOLTED BACK DOWN THE SLOPE TO MY HOUSE so fast I almost tripped and went ass over on the sidewalk. I windmilled one arm, managed to stay on my feet and kept running.

The other hand stayed in my pocket, to make sure my phone didn't go astray. The last thing I needed right now was to have to stop and look for it. Again.

"You know where she is?" I called out when I was within shouting distance of Oaklyn and Gran. They both stood near Gran's old VW beetle, waiting anxiously.

Like Gran, the vehicle was brightly coloured, decorated with rainbows and flowers. With any luck, it actually ran.

"We're only guessing," Oaklyn said. "Gran thinks she took a bus there."

I climbed into the back when Gran moved the seat forward for me. My knees were almost up to my chin, but I fastened my seat belt. "Let's go then."

Oaklyn sat in front of me and Gran drove. Probably the same way she rode a skateboard, taking the corners too fast and almost skidding around.

I grabbed hold of the handle and held on for dear life. This must be how a puck felt, sliding around the ice and taking hits from every angle. And I thought Blake's driving was bad.

"Slow down, Gran!" Oaklyn said after a particularly tight bend.

"If you think this is fast, wait until I get out on the highway," Gran said gleefully.

It was nice knowing you, I silently told my balls. My stomach was trying pretty hard to leave too, as was my last meal. If we didn't get there soon, I was going to be sick in the back of her car.

I focused on breathing and looking out the window while we roared through Lowball Bay, with me squashed like a ball on the back seat.

If the guys could see me now, they'd laugh their heads off. I'd flip them all the bird and remind them this was important. I hoped like hell Gran was right and Cadence was where she thought she was.

After several hours of being scrunched up, doubled in over myself—okay, maybe ten minutes—Gran skidded to a stop outside her old house.

Her and Oaklyn flung open the doors and started to hurry away.

I tapped on the window with my knuckles. "Little help here!"

Oaklyn turned and trotted back. "I'm so sorry!" She wrenched open the door and folded the front seat so I could carefully unwind myself and get out.

"It's okay. I'm sure all of my internal organs will go back where they belong in a minute or two." I shook out my arms and legs and followed them to the small house.

"You really think she's in there?" Oaklyn eyed the front door doubtfully.

"I gave her a key," Gran said. "It makes sense to me that she'd come here and use it. Where else would she go?"

I wouldn't have been surprised if she went back to Highball Creek, but this was a logical possibility.

"I guess we should find out," Oaklyn said. She pulled out her own key and slid it into the lock.

I half expected it to get stuck, or not work, but it turned easily and the door opened.

"Cadence?" Oaklyn called out. She stepped inside and started to look around. "What if she's not here?"

"She's here," I said. I pointed to where the teenager's backpack lay on a vintage dining table. "At least, her bag is."

"If this was *Goldilocks and the Three Bears,* she'd be asleep in her room," Gran said.

"I'll check there," Oaklyn said.

"I'll come with you." I put a hand lightly on her shoulder and followed her down to the end of the short corridor.

Cadence wasn't asleep. She sat in the middle of her bed, earbuds in, grooving to music so loud I could hear some of it.

"And that's where I draw the line, right there in the dirt," she sang loudly and off-key.

"It would seem she also likes Clint Stone," I said approvingly.

Oaklyn glanced at me, then back to Cadence. She stepped over to her and waved a hand in front of her face.

Cadence startled violently, throwing herself

against the pillows that lay between her and the heavy timber headboard.

If it wasn't completely inappropriate, I'd imagine what it would be like with Oaklyn gripping onto the headboard while I fucked her from behind.

Of course it was inappropriate, so I'd think about that later. And by think about it, I meant act it out when we got home.

Apparently my balls survived the car right here after all. Bonus.

"What the fuck?" Cadence pulled out her earbuds and stared at us. "You scared the shit out of me."

"You scared the shit out of us," Oaklyn told her. "Taking off like that. You could have been anywhere. I was scared we'd never see you again."

"You're seeing me now," Cadence said. "As you can see, I'm fine. Not that you give a shit."

Her words hit Oaklyn straight in the heart, I saw that in her blue eyes. So much hurt. So much regret.

"I give a shit," Oaklyn whispered. "Cadence, I love you. A lot. All I want is to be able to give you a good, solid home. One that you can come back to after school every afternoon, knowing there'll be people who care about you. Who love you. Who are never going to walk out on you."

She swallowed hard. Her eyes glazed. She was obviously thinking about the past, like a wound that hadn't fully closed, but was now bleeding around the edges. She was trying to stem the flow, but it was sitting right at the surface. Maybe in a place she hadn't let it be before.

This was a demon she hadn't dealt with and put aside.

I understood then the full extent of what Oaklyn felt right then. Her father walked out and never came back. Cadence might have done the same thing. The memories that brought back, they'd sting like hell.

On top of that, she was scared for her sister. I decided then and there to make it my mission in life to make sure she never felt like that again. I'd be her rock.

If she needed me to be, I'd be a big fucking boulder. Or a mountain. Or a whole damn planet. Whatever it took to let her see she could put her feet on the ground and keep them there, because the earth wasn't going to shake under her anymore.

I wanted the same for Cadence too. Between us and Gran, we could give them what they needed. And then some.

"You didn't want me," Cadence said stubbornly. "Your mother hates me, Gran said so. I heard you talking that night. You're not going to choose me over her."

Her eyes shone with tears, but she blinked them away fiercely. She wanted to be a badass like her sister, but sitting there on the bed with the pale purple duvet, she looked like the vulnerable sixteen-year-old she was.

I pictured Oaklyn on her own bed at that age, dealing with finding out she had a sister. She didn't have as many people around her as Cadence did now. A wave of sadness for young Oaklyn passed over me. She must have felt so alone. So isolated she spent the next sixteen years holding herself apart from everyone else.

Until a brave, young knight happened upon the beautiful princess and tore down all of those walls to reach her. To gather her up in his arms and carry her away into the beautiful sunset.

Okay, I hadn't torn down all of her walls, but I made a dent in them. I'd spend the rest of my life working on all of the other bricks. Carrying her off into the sunset was also something I planned on doing, very soon. After we settled things here.

"Sweetie." Oaklyn sat on the side of the bed beside her. "My mother has her own issues, but those are with our father, not with you or me. She wants to meet you. I know she's going to love you as much as I do. As much as Nate does, right Nate?"

"No question," I said easily. "You two are my girls. Unless either of you support the Toronto Maple Leafs. Then we might have some discussing to do."

I was joking, of course. Mostly. I didn't care which hockey team they supported, as long as they supported me. Although, supporting the Sea Dragons would make life easier.

We'd figure out those details later. When I got them both jerseys for my team. Oaklyn would look adorable with my number—six—on her back.

"Seattle Krakens," Cadence said stubbornly. Her backpack had their logo on it. It was the right sport at least.

I rubbed my chin. "It seems like I have some work to do after all." Starting with a new backpack.

Oaklyn shook her head at me.

I shrugged and grinned before she turned back to her sister.

"I'm sorry if I did anything to make you feel unwanted." She put a hand on Cadence's. "I was worried you might have felt more at home in Highball Creek." She drew her lower lip between her teeth and bit down.

I wished I was the one doing the biting. What can I say, she did it for me.

Cadence shrugged. "I liked it there, but I like Lowball Bay too. I can talk to Lucy and Tessa from here any time."

"You don't want to go back there and stay?" Oaklyn asked tentatively. "Or somewhere else there's kids your age?"

"Nate said we could go back and visit sometimes," Cadence said. She seemed to be challenging us to deny that. Of course I wouldn't. I'd meant what I said.

"Of course we can," I said. "Maybe we could get a place up there and spend the off-season swimming in the creek." A cute little cottage with extra rooms for any future foster kids. Or adopted ones. We could fill the place with laughter and fun. And a whole lot of love. That sounded pretty damn perfect to me.

"Farming cranberries?" Cadence asked. She looked doubtful, like she wasn't sure if that was something she wanted or not. If she was teasing, I'd have to be sure never to play poker with her. Her poker face was top-notch.

On the other hand, I should introduce her to the guys who did play. She'd enjoy taking their money. And I'd enjoy watching her do it.

"If my girl wants a cranberry farm, then I'll buy her a cranberry farm," I said.

"Can I come?" Gran said, peering around my bicep.

"I'm not sure Highball Creek is ready for you Gran," I said. "But of course you can. You'll give the twins a run for their money." Chip and Hank would adore her. Who would follow who into trouble though? They'd probably all hold hands and skip off together.

Jamie was going to lose her mind. I was here for every moment of it.

"Are you ready to come home?" Oaklyn asked Cadence gently.

"I guess," Cadence said. "I'm getting hungry and there's only cans of mushrooms and daiquiri mix in the kitchen."

"Oh, I forgot my daiquiri mix!" Gran darted off.

I grinned and offered a hand to each of my girls. "Let's get out of here then."

"We're going to have to call Kymmie and make

another appointment," Oaklyn said, looking anxious again.

"That part will be a piece of cake," I said. "If Cadence wants to live with us, then it should be a done deal."

It should be, but if word got out that she'd run away, that would complicate the situation.

Chapter Twenty-Nine

Oaklyn

"THESE SEATS ARE AMAZING." CADENCE PLOPPED down beside me.

The tunnel was immediately to her right, behind the plexiglass, with only that between us and the ice. We could have sat in the team box, invited there by Andi, but Cadence wanted to sit closer to the game.

Of course, Nate was only too happy to make it happen.

"Yeah, they're good," I said absently. Three days had passed since Cadence's meeting with Kymmie. I'd hoped to hear back by now, but Kymmie had a family emergency back home in Salt Lake City. It seemed no one else was available to make a decision on her case.

So we waited. I got more and more anxious with each passing day.

Cadence elbowed me in the arm. "They're more than good, Oaks."

She'd taken to calling me by the nickname my mother gave me. Like I hoped, they got along well, having bonded over a mutual enjoyment of super-hero movies. It turned out, Nate enjoyed them too, so the three of them would sit and watch while Gran and I played poker or Monopoly nearby.

When Mom went back to Seattle, we all went to the airport to wave her off and shed a tear. And in Nate's case, to board a different plane with his team to head to Florida.

He arrived home late last night and spent the day resting for tonight's home game. After giving me three amazing orgasms. I was definitely not neglected in that department. Or any others, for that matter. He was unwaveringly sweet and attentive, and didn't bring me any more flowers.

I smiled. "Okay, they're better than good. They're very good."

She elbowed me again. "They're incredible. We can see everything from here. Look, the team is coming!" She dangled over the side, offering a fist bump to all of the guys as they walked past, led by Flynn Weston.

Cam North was right behind him. Then Blake Eastwood, his hands to either side, like he was a penguin. He stopped to fist bump Cadence before waddling on.

"Don't mind him, he has a few screws loose," Nate called up to us.

"More than a few." Zack Reed followed Nate out. He looked like he might walk past, but stopped and tapped his gloved fist against Cadence's hand before continuing on.

Nate looked surprised, but shrugged and hurried out with the rest of the team.

"That was awesome," Cadence breathed.

"Are you considering changing your loyalty to the Sea Dragons?" I teased.

She looked over to me slowly. "Maybe. That depends."

"On what?" I asked.

She shrugged. "I don't know. Stuff."

That was about all I was going to get from her, so I didn't press. Now she was living with me and Nate, she'd be socializing with guys from the team when they came over for dinner or parties. They'd all have a chance to win her over in person.

The same couldn't be said for any other players on the continent. Did that give them an unfair advantage? Maybe, but it was what it was. Family looked after family.

We watched as the guys warmed up, the Sea Dragons and the Stickville Danglers, who'd come to play as the away team tonight.

"You've never been to a professional hockey game before?" I asked.

Cadence drew back in on herself a little. "Mom was the one who likes hockey. Dad didn't. For some reason, that meant we didn't get to go. It was like she thought he'd be upset or something."

"Was it often like that?" I asked.

"Walking on eggshells? Yeah. I get why now though." She half smiled as Blake and the opposing goalie waltzed around the ice for a few moments. "Mom was always worried he'd leave. If she ever did anything he didn't like, he got real quiet. And she got real nervous. And then he'd buy her flowers and everything would go back to normal."

That sounded familiar. Until she mentioned it, I'd forgotten how quiet Dad used to get, and how on edge it made Mom. At some point, my mind had painted the picture of a perfect family, right up until the moment I discovered Cadence's existence. But it wasn't good and it hadn't been for a long time. Maybe all my life.

When you were living it, it was harder to see, but now it was so obvious. It might have been better if he left years earlier. Mom and I could have gotten on with our lives sooner.

"I'm sorry you went through that," I said. "And that your mother went through that."

Yes, Rebecca knew about my mother, but no one deserved to spend their days worrying that their partner might disappear in the night. Instead, Cadence lost both of them at the same time and at the same age I was when my father left. That was doubly bad.

"I'm glad you came to find me." I put my hand on hers. "I know I didn't make things easy, but I think we're on the right track now. We can put the past behind us and move on."

I booked therapy sessions for Cadence, with the counsellor who worked for the team. They also worked with any family members who needed their support. Something I'd forever be grateful for.

"I'm glad I did too," she said. "Plan B was hitchhiking to Disney World and trying to get a job dressing up as Sleeping Beauty."

"That's a solid Plan B," I said. "But I like Plan A better."

"Me too." She leaned against me, her head on my shoulder before straightening back up again. "Plan C was heading out to a ranch and becoming a cowgirl."

"Also a solid plan," I said with a nod. "I could have hooked you up with a gig at Cornball Ranch. It's up in the mountains, north of Highball Creek. A former client of mine owns the place." She'd run away from her wedding and fell in love with a cowboy, but that was a whole other story.

"You don't want me to go, do you?" Cadence looked anxious suddenly.

"Of *course* not." I put my arm around her shoulders and held her close. "You have to finish school first. Then if you want to go to college, or travel, or get a job or whatever, I hope you'll always come home to me and Nate." I found tears pooling in the corners of my eyes.

"You can't get rid of me easily," she said, sniffing. "Once social services says I can stay, you're stuck with me."

"I wouldn't have it any other way," I assured her.

Now if they'd just contact us, we could settle into this new normal.

"There you are." Gran flopped into the seat on

the other side of me, carrying a huge tub of popcorn in one hand and a beer in the other. "Well, aren't these awesome seats?"

She wore an oversized Sea Dragons jersey over bright orange leggings that contrasted with her lime green bucket hat and earrings shaped like octopuses.

If she was trying to stand out, she succeeded. Like she always did. I doubted 'blending in' was even in her vocabulary. And if it was, it was probably considered a swear word. The kind that never gets said out loud, for fear of having your mouth washed out with soap, or whatever people used to do back in the dark ages.

"They're the best." Cadence mopped at her eyes.

"You're the best," I said.

"Darn tootin' I am," Gran agreed. She toasted me with her beer and grinned, as though the compliment was about her.

I snorted softly. "You too." She was over the top, but I wouldn't have her any other way. Life without her would be boring anyway. She always kept me guessing, but she kept us all laughing as well. Everyone should have someone like her in their lives.

I startled as my phone vibrated in my back pocket.

Was that Kymmie? It wasn't quite four in the

afternoon in Utah. Working hours for her if she was able to sneak in some work while she was tending to her family. I certainly didn't expect her to take time away from that to contact us, but if she had I'd be eternally grateful. Soon, we'd be having a double celly—the Sea Dragons' win, and knowing Cadence could stay with us. Right?

My heart raced and my palms sweated. Trembling, I reached for my phone and slid it out of my pocket.

I glanced at the screen. My heart sank. I pressed on it to answer the call and put the phone to my ear.

"Lacey, hey, how's things?" I hadn't expected to hear from the woman whose job I was keeping warm while she was on maternity leave. I hoped everything was okay with her and the baby. I hadn't met him, but I'd seen photos and he was adorable. Like all babies were.

That familiar pang was still there in my chest, but it wasn't as painful as it used to be. Not when I knew my future might include babies after all. But if it didn't, that was okay too. I wasn't going to say no to any kid who needed us, whatever their age.

"Oaklyn! I'm so sorry to call late, I just got the baby to sleep. I wanted to let you know I'm coming back to work early. I'll be back there in a week."

"That's great," I said with no enthusiasm. I hadn't had a chance to tell Nate about any of that yet. To be honest, I'd forgotten. I was thinking about Cadence and waiting for Kymmie's call.

"It is!" she said. "I love being a mom, but I can't wait to get back to work. We've talked about it, and since Jason can work from home, he's going to be the stay-at-home daddy. It's so perfect."

"That's wonderful," I said. "I know everyone here has missed you a lot." My gaze wandered to the ice as the guys were ready for puck drop. Flynn was first to take possession of the puck, driving it deep into offensive territory.

"I've missed them too," she said. "Thank you so much for stepping in for me. You're the best." She sounded so sincere and sweet. Honestly, she was both of those things, which made me feel horrible for not being excited for her.

Of course she was happy to get back to work. She was the kind of person who enjoyed being active and around people, and the arena was a lovely work environment. Thanks to Andi Welling for making everyone feel included and part of the family.

Her owning the team was one of the best things that ever happened to the Sea Dragons, not to mention to Cam North. Although, those two were always destined to find each other. The same way Nate and I were destined to be together. Fate would have found a way, somehow.

"Yeah, I'm sure you do." I didn't feel much like the best right now. I felt like the cards were still up in the air, slowly floating to the ground one by one. As one landed, I was still waiting for fifty more of them to settle.

"I'll let you enjoy your night then," she said. "Thanks again. Byeee!"

"Goodbye," I said into the silence after the phone clicked, indicating she'd ended the call.

"Is everything okay?" Gran asked.

I put my phone away and forced a smile. "Of course. Everything is just fine."

I sat back and tried to focus on the game while my mind was miles away. Was a stable life something unattainable for me after all?

Or was it a thing I could still spend the rest of my life searching for and never find? Even with Nate.

Chapter Thirty

Nate

"Okay, what's up?"

Oaklyn hardly said a word all the way home and while we were getting ready for bed.

We'd beaten the Danglers five to three, had a quick celly in the locker room before we'd all headed home. Cadence and Gran were both buzzing with excitement, especially Cadence. I introduced her to some of the guys after the game. After we got clean and didn't smell like feet.

Blake made a new fan of her by giving her a signed puck. The moment was caught on camera by Alice North to be shared on the team's social media channels.

Through all of that, Oaklyn stayed back, her expression apprehensive, even on edge. The guys could be a lot, especially Blake, but I didn't think that was what was on her mind. I tried to get a chance to talk to her, but it wasn't until we lay in bed, me spooning her that I was able to.

"I can tell something is bothering you," I said. "You know you can talk to me about anything, right?"

"I know," she whispered. "I just don't know how to... Where to start."

"My father used to say the best place to start was at the beginning." I placed a hand on her hip and under the hem of her pajama shirt. Just enough to trace circles on her warm, smooth skin with the pad of my thumb.

She sighed softly. "I guess that's as good a place as any." She was silent for a few moments. So long I thought she'd fallen asleep.

"You know the job at the arena was only temporary, right?"

My thumb stopped mid-circle. "It was?"

The staff gym had been part of the facility for a long time, but Andi had it renovated. Cam wanted to see it, knowing it was important to her and I'd gone along for shits and giggles. That was when I met Oaklyn. And fell head over skates for her.

I assumed she was new. If she'd been there for a

long time, I would have noticed her. There was another woman there instead, wasn't there? Lindsay? Leslie?

"Just while Lacey was on leave to have her baby," Oaklyn said. "She's coming back next week."

Her words were like a kick right in the left nut. I thought we'd drive to work together whenever we started at the same time. We could have lunch together in the arena café when time allowed. Maybe sneak off for a quickie in one of the storage rooms.

"When were you going to tell me this?" I asked.

She rolled over to face me, illuminated by the glow of a streetlight that slanted through the curtains. "I've been trying to think of how to say it. My original plan was to move on when I was finished there."

"And by move on, you mean...?" My mouth was suddenly dry.

"Move on," she said again. "Leave Lowball Bay. Go somewhere else and see how I like it there."

"That was your original plan," I said. "Up until... when?" Did I really want the answer to that?

She swallowed audibly. "Up until you kissed me, and Chip and Hank pushed us in the creek. That was when I knew I couldn't walk away."

That kiss would live in my head, rent free. for the

rest of my life. The moment our lips met, the entire universe aligned. Maybe a chorus of angels came out to sing, or got their wings or something.

Whatever it was, it cemented what I already knew. She and I were destined to be together. If there was a higher power, they planned this centuries ago. We were as inevitable as the sun rising. Being pushed into that freezing water hadn't dulled the heat that surged through me from that kiss. If anything, it ignited harder and hotter.

After all, cold water does make blood pump faster. I could do with a cold shower now, it might help to engage my brain better. To make sense of everything that happened before and after that kiss.

"We were trying to foster Cadence before that," I said slowly.

Even then, she was thinking of ending things? I knew the engagement was fake, but apparently it was even more of a sham than I thought. Or had been, before that kiss. What else was a sham?

"I know," she whispered. "I figured you and Gran would have taken custody of her."

A long, heavy silence fell after those words.

That was a lot to process. She'd really considered leaving her sister with her grandmother and me? Move to another part of the country and...then what?

Forget we existed? Maybe send a Christmas card once in a while, to remind us she was alive? Abandon her sister who still needed her, even when she was trying to be a badass teenager? It was likely Cadence would always need her in one capacity or another. They were family after all. Gran and I were awesome, but would we have been enough, just the two of us? We'd try, but neither of us were Oaklyn.

"You would have waited until we were approved to foster her and then you would have walked away?" I couldn't quite believe what I was hearing.

"I thought I could," she admitted. "Because that's what I've always done. Walked away. Then I realized I couldn't walk away from her or you. It was terrifying. I was getting so attached to both of you. It took the fall into the water to realize I'd already fallen. There was no going back then, not even if I wanted to."

"You don't want to, right?" I asked. Not insecure, but firm.

If she thought I was letting her turn her back on me now, she'd have to think again. If she left the city, I'd pack up and follow her. Better yet, I'd tie her to my bed before she could leave. And keep her like that until she changed her mind.

Yes, I know there are laws against that, but if she

was planning to walk away, I'd take desperate measures. She was mine and I wasn't letting her go without a hell of a fight.

"There's nowhere in the world I'd rather be," she said. "Lacey deciding to come back early was a surprise, but I'll figure out something else. It's time I committed to something more permanent."

"What do you want to do?" I asked. I couldn't keep the relief out of my voice. Didn't even try. Of course she wanted to stay. I shouldn't have doubted that.

Knowing there was a time when she had her doubts wasn't really a surprise. I knew she initially wasn't as sure of us as I was, but now I knew what was going through her head at the time. And why.

She must have struggled with all of that so much, but kept silent because of Cadence. Because she wanted to make a home for her, even if she wasn't part of it. Because her sister's happiness was more important to her than her own.

I made a note to make sure she put herself first once in a while. Or all the time. If she didn't book her own spa days and breaks, I'd book them for her. For us. I could use a spa day once in a while. What? I like facials, okay? Every guy should have them, if they wanted to.

She gave a short laugh. "I don't know. I guess I could take personal clients. I could build my business as a personal trainer."

I rolled her over, pinned her hands above her head and straddled her hips. "Are you going to get up close and personal with other men?" I touched the tip of my nose to hers.

"Not as up close and personal as this," she said.

"Good," I growled playfully. "Because no one gets personal as puck with you except me." I slanted my mouth and slammed it down to hers.

She wrapped her arms around my neck and her legs around my hips, holding me close while I ground my cock against her pussy, only thin pajama fabric between us. In half a heartbeat I was harder than a rock. Wanting nothing but to slide inside her and show her how I felt about her.

"I don't want to get this personal with anyone else," she whispered against my mouth.

"Me either." I pushed up the front of her pajama shirt and proceeded to get personal with her breasts, teasing and sucking her nipples until they were hard and tight.

She slipped her hand between us, into my pajama pants and wrapped it around my length. Her touch was almost enough to send me over the edge then and there. But I had no intention of rushing.

I gently pulled away from her, rolled off her just enough to remove all of the offending clothing between us and parted her beautiful thighs to dive down between them. Carefully and thoroughly, I got personal with my tongue on her pussy, licking and sucking until she shattered beautifully.

"That's the first of many tonight," I told her. Even though it was probably morning by now. I didn't care, I wasn't done, not by a long way.

"Is it really?" she said with a smile. "Are you sure about that?"

"It absolutely is, and I absolutely am," I agreed. I'd never been more sure about anything. All I wanted to do in life was make her feel good. Over and over and over again. Until she was satisfied and exhausted in the best way possible.

I went back to work, enjoying the taste of her and her breathy little moans until she turned around, wrapping her lips around my cock while I lapped at her.

"Fucking hell woman, your mouth is incredible," I whispered. Somehow she knew exactly what I liked and how I liked it. Just the right angle, and pressure.

The perfect amount of teasing with the tip of her tongue.

"No, yours," she said with a laugh before taking me into the back of her throat and sucking harder.

"If you can talk, I'm not working hard enough," I told her. With my mouth and fingers, I drove her to the edge again, until all that was coming out of her mouth were pants and moans, and her tongue teasing me. She shattered again, against my mouth, almost taking me with her.

I turned us back around, lay beside her and pulled her leg over my hip before sliding deep inside her.

"You were made for me," I told her. "The perfect fit. So tight." I moved inside her slowly, wanting to savor every moment.

We had the rest of our lives to do this, but I'd never take a second of it for granted. Not with her body and certainly not with her heart.

"I love you," she whispered, right back on the edge again.

"I love you too, cupcake," I said. "Why don't you take charge for a while?" I rolled us over until she was straddling me, her glorious breasts on full display.

"What makes you think I need practice telling men what to do?" she teased.

She placed her hands on my chest and rose and fell slowly, teasing and drawing the pleasure out for both of us.

I laughed softly. "I guess you don't." Then I was coming again and so was she. Shattering together in perfect unison, bodies sliding against each other, slick with fresh sweat from the most perfect work out of all. Making love to each other. Knowing we had forever. She was never leaving me and I was never leaving her.

But after we had a quick shower, cleaned each other up and curled up back in bed I remembered there were still two pieces of the puzzle left to put in place. One of those, I could take care of tomorrow.

If Oaklyn and Cadence would let me.

Chapter Thirty-One

Oaklyn

"What are you up to?" I asked, eyeing Nate.

He was absolutely gorgeous that day, in dark jeans and a black sweater. I could hardly believe he was interested in me at all, much less that we were together. After explaining everything the other night, I felt like a weight was lifted off me. I could enjoy living my life in a way I hadn't let myself do before.

For once, I was actually looking forward to the future.

If only Kymmie would call.

"What makes you think I'm up to anything?" He offered both of his arms, one to me and one to Cadence.

"The expression on your face," I told him. "And

the way you told us both to get in the car because you're taking us to town. On a Monday afternoon."

"The way you didn't answer Oaklyn when she asked why," Cadence said. She didn't seem to mind being dragged away from homework for a few hours.

"That too," I agreed. "All of that adds up to you being up to something."

"Fine, I'm up to something," he said with a grin. "You'll find out in a moment. Don't worry, you're both going to like it."

"Are we getting clam chowder?" Cadence asked hopefully.

"We can get that after," Nate assured her. "We have something important to do first."

He led us down the sidewalk about fifty feet until we stopped in front of a jewelry store.

"Nate..." I said carefully. "I don't need a ring." I glanced over to Cadence.

"I know the engagement is fake," she said, as though we were being obtuse. "You guys did that for me, right? So that social services lady would think you were together and make it easier for me to stay with you."

"Cadence..." I was now speaking to her carefully.

"It's okay," she said quickly. "I think it's kinda

sweet. That you pretend something like that because you wanted me around that much."

"We did, and we do," I assured her. Having another secret out in the open was a relief. Especially knowing it was the last one. After this, I wasn't keeping anything from either of them.

"Yes, we do," Nate agreed. "But this isn't an engagement ring. Yet. When I give you one of those, I'll be down on one knee, asking you to be my wife. This is a promise ring. One for each of you. It's my promise to you. That I'll never walk away from either of you. Let's go in so you can have a look."

I couldn't take a step, I was too busy staring at him. "Nathaniel David Southwell, that might be the sweetest thing I ever heard."

He actually blushed. "If you think that's sweet, then you better buckle up, buttercup. I have a whole lifetime of this in store for you. Come on, cupcake." He tugged me forward through the door and into the store.

"Have a look around and see if there's anything you'd like," he said. He spread his hands to gesture all the way around the glittering cabinets full of what looked like very expensive jewelry.

"I'm not much of a ring person," Cadence said,

but she wandered off to look at the display of silver rings.

"You don't have to do this, you know," I told him. "I know you'll never walk away from us."

"I want to," he said. "The next time we play a home game, I want you wearing my jersey and my ring. A promise ring for now. Some day, a wedding ring."

"If you make me cry..." I warned. But a tear already trickled down my cheek. He wiped it away with the pad of his thumb.

He leaned in and whispered. "I like making you wet, no matter what part of you it is."

"You're a brat," I whispered back.

He chuckled. "Yeah, but I'm your brat. Now, go and choose a ring." He slapped my ass, making me jump.

"Yes sir," I teased. I loved the way his eyes darkened when I said that, and while he watched me browse the selection of shining rings.

"I think I like this one." I tapped the glass right above one ring in particular.

The store assistant unlocked the display and pulled out the tray to give me a closer look. "You can try it on if you like."

I pulled it out of the velvet display case and slid

it onto the ring finger of my right hand. "It fits perfectly." Made of yellow, white and rose gold, the ring consisted of three interlocking circles, one of each of the metals.

"I found one I—" Cadence stopped, her hand held out towards us. On her finger was a ring in the same design of mine, but with all three sections in silver.

"One circle for each of you and one for me," Nate said.

"That's what I was thinking," I said softly. "Three very different people, but we've all come together as a family." If I kept on going on like that, I was going to end up sobbing. "And apparently, Cadence and I have the same taste in rings."

"That's because we're both awesome," Cadence said. She looked a bit teary herself. "Can I have this one, please?"

"Absolutely," Nate agreed. "I'll have them ring up both of them. Pun totally intended."

Cadence and I exchanged glances, matching eye rolls and groaned. Then we both burst out laughing.

The more I got to know her, the more I discovered how alike we were. We had a similar sense of humour, and appreciation for vintage clothes. And we both enjoyed listening to Clint Stone, and Jack Clatterbuck, two of Nate's favorite singers.

We might never agree on watching social media reels, but that was okay. She could have her hot boy videos and I'd stick to watching funny animal ones.

My smile faded when my phone rang in my pocket. For a while, I'd forgotten all about Kymmie and the fact she could call any day now.

My stomach got slightly nauseous as I pulled out my phone and looked at the screen.

"It's Kymmie." I hesitated for a heartbeat before I tapped to answer the call and put it to my ear. I nodded while I listened to her, responding with vague words here and there, before relaying the conversation to Nate and Cadence.

"They've made a decision," I said slowly. "They've agreed to let us foster Cadence. In fact, Kymmie was so impressed with us, she's hoping we can take on another couple of kids."

"Life just got a whole lot more fun," Nate said.

I couldn't argue with that. I was too busy thinking about what we need to help our growing family settle in.

Epilogue

Oaklyn

"IT'S THE PERFECT DAY FOR A POOL PARTY," ANDI remarked. She sat on one side of me on a lounger, carefully in the shade of an umbrella.

"It is," I agreed. I toyed with the ring on my left hand. Even after a month, it felt strange to have a wedding band there. Strange in a good way though. After a couple of years of patience, Nate finally got down on one knee and proposed.

Of course I said yes, but it wasn't the last time that day I cried. Dropping Cadence off at the dormitory of her school of choice, Snowball College, up in the mountains, came with another bucket of tears.

We'd become close since she turned up on my doorstep. Part of me wanted to keep her in Lowball

Bay, but I knew she was ready to go out on her own, even if I wasn't.

Nate reminded me of the reason why we fostered all the kids that we had. Because it was our job to help them find their wings. So they could soar and have amazing lives, but know they'd have somewhere to land if they needed it.

I looked to where he sat on the other side of the pool, talking to his brother, Rhys. We finally managed to convince him to take a few hours off, come over and bring his kids to hang out and play with the others. Rhys looked exhausted, but the kids seemed to be having the time of their lives. Whatever the brothers were talking about, it looked intense. No doubt Nate would tell me all about it later. There were no secrets between us anymore.

A couple of feet away from Nate, Flynn sat drinking a brightly coloured cocktail from a fancy glass. Or at least, he had the straw in his mouth. His eyes were on Valentina, who wore a bikini and stood talking and laughing with Jamie.

Nate's sister brought her family from Highball Creek for the party. I couldn't hear what they were saying either, but whatever it was, it made Flynn frown.

"It looks to me like married life agrees with you," Alice said from the other side of me. "I'm happy for you both." She clutched a folded sheet of paper in her hand.

"Another love letter from your secret admirer? You might be next to tie the knot." I gave her a sly smile.

She blushed. "It is, but I'm going to go out of my mind before I—" She stopped mid-sentence to stare in the direction of the second level of the house.

I followed her gaze, to where Blake stood on one of the upper balconies. He was grinning and climbing onto the thick stone railing.

Alice shot to her feet and pushed her sunglasses off her face. "What the hell do you think you're doing?" she demanded.

He grinned bigger. "I'm going to jump into the pool."

"The hell you are!" She placed her fists on her hips. "Get down from there before you injure yourself." Under her breath she added, "Stupid fucking man!"

"If you insist," Blake called down. He steadied himself on the railing, hands out to either side. He looked down toward the pool, judging the angle he'd have to make in order to hit the water and not the pool deck.

"I can't watch," Alice groaned. She put a hand over her face as Blake bent his knees and started to jump.

A second or two later, we were all covered in a wave of water which accompanied the resounding splash of him hitting the center of the pool.

The whole party erupted in a loud cheer, followed by chanting. "Blake! Blake! Blake!"

Alice lowered her hand and shook her head. "Stop encouraging him. That man is going to be the absolute death of me. If he's not the death of himself first."

I exchanged glances with Andi, who nodded and smiled. Evidently she picked up on the same vibe too. Alice and Blake would be adorable together. If they both survived long enough to see that themselves.

Things were definitely going to be interesting with the Lowball Bay Sea Dragons for the next while.

Thank you for reading! If you'd love a glimpse into

the future of Nate and Oaklyn, you can download their bonus scene here.

Next up in the Sea Dragon's world is Blake and Alice's story. You can find that here.

About the Author

Freya M. Love writes steamy romantic comedies with guys we like to swoon over and women we can relate to. All wrapped up with a snort-worthy bow that comes with no guarantee you won't spit out your drink.

Join the fun of Freya's Lovlies on Facebook! Join!
Subscribe to my Newsletter.
Follow me on Pinterest.
Follow me on TikTok.
Follow me on Amazon.
Follow me on Bookbub.

Also by Freya M. Love

Lowball Bay Sea Dragons

Not the Puck Bunny

Personal as Puck

Influential as Puck

For the Love of Puck